BEACON STREET GIRLS

This book belongs to:

VERITAS AMICITIA GAUDIUM
truth friendship fun!

TM

CR

BEACON STREET GIRLS

lake rescue

First Edition

Special thanks to Dr. Lilian Cheung—D.Sc., R.D., Director of Health Promotion &
Communication, Department of Nutrition, Harvard School of Public Health;
Mavis Jukes—teacher and best-selling author: *Be Healthy! It's a Girl Thing: Food,
Fitness, and Feeling Great*; Dr. Catherine Steiner-Adair—Ed.D., Clinical Instructor,
Department of Psychiatry, Harvard Medical School, and co-author of *Full of
Ourselves: A Wellness Curriculum to Advance Girl Power, Health & Leadership*;
Jill Zimmerman Rutledge—M.S.W., and author of *Dealing with the Stuff That
Makes Life Tough: The 10 Things That Stress Girls Out and
How to Cope with Them*; and to Sarah Wanger—teen reader.

Series Editor: Roberta MacPhee
Art Direction: Pamela M. Esty
Book Design: Dina Barsky
Illustration: Pamela M. Esty
Cover photograph: Digital composition

Produced by B*tween Productions, Inc.
1666 Massachusetts Avenue, Suite 17
Lexington, MA 02420

ISBN: 0-9758511-3-6

CIP data is available at the Library of Congress
10 9 8 7 6 5 4 3 2 1

Printed in the U.S.A.

CR

Visit the Beacon Street Girls at: www.beaconstreetgirls.com

PART ONE

LIONS AND SPIDERS AND BEARS,
OH MY!

CR

CHAPTER 1

ℭ

CAMP WHERE?

"CHARLOTTE," Jennifer Robinson, editor of *The Sentinel*, said abruptly. "Can you get this story from Mrs. Fields ready by Friday? She just dropped off information about the trip to Lake Rescue."

"What trip? Lake Rescue? Why would anyone go there?"

Charlotte had been daydreaming about the BSG's magic act in the recent school talent show. Marty had been so cute lying on his back with his little paws up in the air.

The leap from "magic" to being rescued from some lake was more than Charlotte could handle at the moment.

"Oh, that's right ... you're new this year." Jennifer adjusted her funky purple glasses and continued. "Lake Rescue is up in the White Mountain National Forest of New Hampshire. Abigail Adams seventh graders go there every year for, you know, 'the outdoor education experience.' So this has to go in Friday's paper. Mrs. Fields will give you all the gory details tomorrow."

"I hope so." Charlotte stared intently at the stack of papers in front of her.

"Oh, I forgot. Can you ask Isabel to do a cartoon about the trip?"

"Sure. I'll call her tonight."

Mountains? Lakes? Outdoor education adventure? Charlotte had to take a few deep breaths to calm down. The possibility of a new adventure was just too exciting. Memories of Australia and Africa flooded her senses. She absolutely loved being outside, camping, hiking, swimming. Was it too cold to swim in the lake? Would they have boats? That would be too cool. She could hardly wait to tell her dad about the trip. Maybe he had already been to New Hampshire.

When she finally gathered her things and made it outside, Charlotte looked around for her friends, but the Abigail Adams school grounds were deserted. She checked her watch again. She wasn't that late. She must have missed everybody by just a couple of minutes.

Charlotte pulled her jacket closer and hurried toward Beacon Street, then crossed over to Corey Hill toward her house.

On impulse, she stopped at Montoya's Bakery for hot chocolate. She figured Nick would probably not be there, but she told herself that she didn't care if he was or not. Once she entered the bakery, the delicious smells of chocolate cookies freshly baked and coffee, which she didn't drink, made her feel warm and cozy inside.

"Two hot chocolates to go, please," Charlotte ordered. She'd take her dad one on the chance that he'd be home to share her news.

"*Hola*, Charlotte," Mrs. Montoya said. "Where are the rest of your *amigas*?" Charlotte loved the way Mrs. Montoya threw in a few Spanish words every now and then. It made Charlotte feel as if she were someplace exotic ... maybe like the Alhambra Palace in Spain. It was supposed to be spectacular ... definitely on her list of must-sees.

"I don't know *where* those girls are," she answered. "I was working on the newspaper and left school late. Avery must have a soccer game. Maeve probably had to baby-sit her brother Sam. I only hope Katani and Isabel are thinking about how we're going to dress for Pajama Day. They are the only ones who know how to sew in our group."

"Ah, yes. Nick told me about that. We never got to wear pajamas to school in my day. It sounds like good fun."

All of a sudden, Charlotte realized that she had been standing there without paying attention to anything. For a minute, she couldn't even remember what they were talking about.

At the sound of Nick's name, Charlotte had felt a little fluttery, but she didn't want Mrs. Montoya to think she had a major crush on her son. She reasoned that Nick was just a friend ... her first real "boy" friend.

"Charlotte," Mrs. Montoya asked, "What are you wearing?"

"Pajamas, funny pajamas." Charlotte breathed a sigh of relief. She didn't want Mrs. Montoya telling her son that something was wrong with her. "It's going to be seriously funny. I can hardly wait. The Beacon Street Girls are all going to dress alike."

Mrs. Montoya raised her eyebrows.

Oh, no. Charlotte's heart skipped a beat. She's going to tell Nick that I'm *muy loca.*

"Like Wee Willie Winkie," Mrs. Montoya began to recite.

Charlotte was relieved, but she missed Mrs. Montoya's reference. "Who's that?"

"You know ... the nursery rhyme, about that funny little

fellow Wee Willie Winkie, upstairs and down, who ran all over town in his nightgown. Surely your mother read …"

"No, not that one," Charlotte sighed. "We just kept reading *Charlotte's Web* over and over."

"With the little spider … that's so nice, Charlotte," Mrs. Montoya responded. She then handed Charlotte the bag with two hot chocolates to go. "Want some biscotti? They are just out of the oven. A couple would go nicely with the cocoa."

Charlotte nodded her head. Montoya's biscotti were famous. People lined up in the morning to get them for breakfast. "Just a couple." She searched her purse for enough money to cover her purchase. The cookies were a good idea. Last time she had looked, the cookie jar was empty.

With hot chocolate and cookies in hand, Charlotte waved good-bye to Mrs. Montoya and walked quickly but carefully toward home. She didn't want the hot chocolates to lose their lids. She could just see herself falling and making a big splat on the street … with kids riding by on their bikes and people staring out of the trolley. She could see the headlines now, "Huge Fall on Beacon Street. Abigail Adams Student Bites the Dust. Hot Chocolate to Blame." My inner journalist comes popping up at the oddest of times, Charlotte thought to herself.

She was totally relieved when she reached the yellow Victorian that was home to the globe-trotting Ramseys. As she set everything down to use her key, she could hear Marty the dog dancing and yelping in excitement on the other side of the door.

The little dog followed her all the way to the kitchen, where she found her dad staring into the cupboards, looking puzzled, as if somehow cookies were supposed to appear by magic.

"Here, Dad, I brought us a treat." Charlotte set the cocoa

cups down, placed the biscotti on a saucer, and plopped down opposite her father at the kitchen table. "I have so much to tell you."

"Should I prepare myself?" Charlotte's dad always had a twinkle in his eyes when he looked at her. Charlotte felt so lucky. Her father was right there when she needed to talk. But he wasn't always in her face either. He gave her lots of private time to write and stare up at the stars. They seemed to have found just the right balance.

She thought of Maeve's father, who was now living apart from the family, and how Maeve's parents would probably be getting a divorce. Of course, Maeve got to see her father on weekends, and Avery flew to Colorado every Christmas and summer to ski and hike with her dad. And they both could email their dads anytime they wanted. But "it's not the same," Maeve had sighed, "when you don't have a dad in the house to help you."

"I love you, Dad," Charlotte said as she dipped the biscotti into the warm, sweet hot chocolate. A deliciously perfect snack, she thought. Charlotte was grateful that she and her dad got along so well—even if he had been a little absent-minded lately.

"Uh-oh, this is going to be worse than I imagined." Mr. Ramsey opened his hot chocolate. He took a big sip, reached for a chocolate biscotti, and dipped the crispy cookie in the cocoa for a couple of seconds before he bit off a chunk.

Charlotte laughed. "No, Dad. Don't worry. No klutz attacks this time. This is *good* news. The entire seventh grade is going to New Hampshire, on an outdoor education adventure. We'll be camping, hiking, who knows what. Now, what do you know about New Hampshire?"

Mr. Ramsey frowned and thought for a minute. "I think

the rattlesnakes may be holing up for the winter, but they do have the biggest spiders in the United States. Ferocious, man-eating spiders and bears. Let's see, and mountain lions too, I believe. No, I am sure of it. I don't think you should go to New Hampshire, Charlotte—too dangerous even for somebody who has fought off an angry rhino in Africa and snorkeled off the Great Barrier Reef. No, I don't think I can allow it."

Her dad loved to tease.

"Remember when that lady gave me that baby koala to hold? He was so unbelievably cute."

"That was a great day," Mr. Ramsey recalled. "I wonder where that photo is of you holding him?"

"That little bear was so soft. He took hold of me the minute the trainer put him in my arms." Charlotte could remember how cuddly the koala was. He was like a big stuffed toy.

"That's a reflex. Koalas hold onto their mothers like that, then hold onto tree limbs so they can feed. I doubt New Hampshire has any koalas or ostriches either, but watch your towel. A bear might like to take a good chomp out of it."

Mr. Ramsey was referring to the time an ostrich was watching them eat breakfast when they were camping in Africa. What that bird was watching for was the opportunity to snatch Charlotte's washrag off their little clothesline. They chased him, but never were able to get it back.

"He's probably still washing his face with it every morning."

They could have gone on with their memories for the rest of the night. How many daughters had traveled all over the world or had so much fun with their fathers? "You'll need some new gear. I can take you and the other BSG shopping for your trip." Mr. Ramsey finished his cookie and got up to put the plates into the dishwasher.

"Like you went shopping for groceries on your way home from work today?" Charlotte grinned.

"Busted. I totally forgot. I guess we might just have to go out to dinner. We'll get a few groceries on the way home. Can't shop when we're hungry." Mr. Ramsey gave his stomach a pat.

Charlotte glanced at her watch. "Give me a few minutes, Dad, OK? I need to ask Isabel about something for the school newspaper."

"Sure. I'll just clean up … don't be long."

"I won't."

Charlotte ran to the Tower where she had left her notebook. Every time she pulled down the stairs and climbed to her favorite hideaway, she thought how lucky she and her dad were to have found the old yellow Victorian. And how cool it was that she and her friends, who weren't friends at the time, found the secret space.

Back in her bedroom, Charlotte logged on, then hit IM, hoping some of the BSG were on.

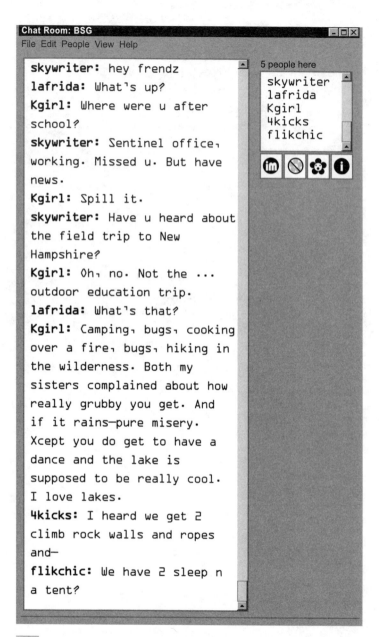

Chat Room: BSG

File Edit People View Help

skywriter: hey frendz
lafrida: What's up?
Kgirl: Where were u after school?
skywriter: Sentinel office, working. Missed u. But have news.
Kgirl: Spill it.
skywriter: Have u heard about the field trip to New Hampshire?
Kgirl: Oh, no. Not the ... outdoor education trip.
lafrida: What's that?
Kgirl: Camping, bugs, cooking over a fire, bugs, hiking in the wilderness. Both my sisters complained about how really grubby you get. And if it rains—pure misery. Xcept you do get to have a dance and the lake is supposed to be really cool. I love lakes.
4kicks: I heard we get 2 climb rock walls and ropes and—
flikchic: We have 2 sleep n a tent?

5 people here

skywriter
lafrida
Kgirl
4kicks
flikchic

4kicks: No, there r cabins.
flikchic: r there bathrooms
please tell me there r
bathrooms?
4kicks: Sure. We're not
backpacking in the wilderness
here.
flikchic: I can't possibly do
n e of that. I'm not going—
I detest spiders of all
kinds.
lafrida: OK that.
Kgirl: I think u have 2.
Unless your parents write an
excuse.
skywriter: u guys! This will
b fun. We'll b n it 2gether.
My dad and I camped all the
time in Africa and Australia.
We had such great adventures.
flikchic: I don't need
adventures. Living 2 places,
putting up with Sam is
plenty of adventure 4 me.
Last night he jumped out
from under my bed with a
water pistol. Besidz I'm a
real city girl.
lafrida: Do boys go too?

5 people here

skywriter
lafrida
Kgirl
4kicks
flikchic

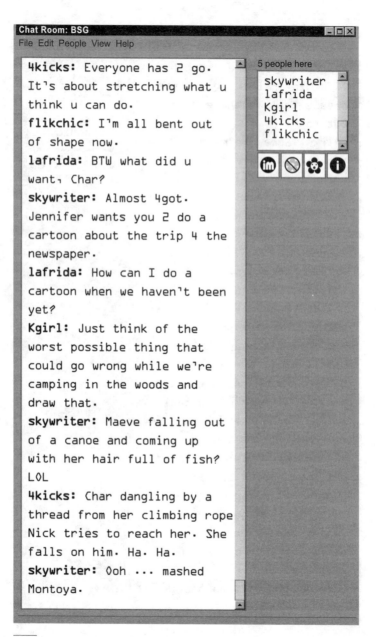

Chat Room: BSG

File Edit People View Help

4kicks: Everyone has 2 go. It's about stretching what u think u can do.

flikchic: I'm all bent out of shape now.

lafrida: BTW what did u want, Char?

skywriter: Almost 4got. Jennifer wants you 2 do a cartoon about the trip 4 the newspaper.

lafrida: How can I do a cartoon when we haven't been yet?

Kgirl: Just think of the worst possible thing that could go wrong while we're camping in the woods and draw that.

skywriter: Maeve falling out of a canoe and coming up with her hair full of fish? LOL

4kicks: Char dangling by a thread from her climbing rope Nick tries to reach her. She falls on him. Ha. Ha.

skywriter: Ooh ... mashed Montoya.

5 people here

skywriter
lafrida
Kgirl
4kicks
flikchic

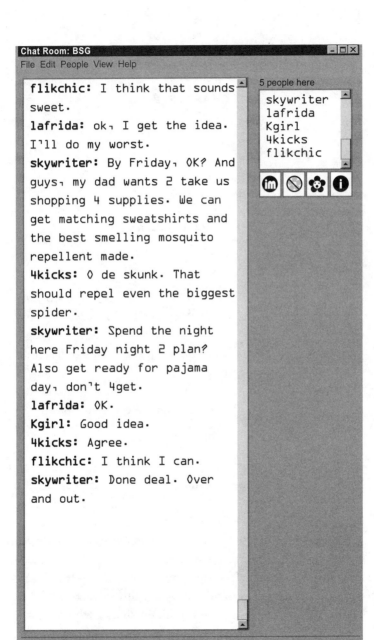

Chat Room: BSG

File　Edit　People　View　Help

5 people here

skywriter
lafrida
Kgirl
4kicks
flikchic

flikchic: I think that sounds sweet.

lafrida: ok, I get the idea. I'll do my worst.

skywriter: By Friday, OK? And guys, my dad wants 2 take us shopping 4 supplies. We can get matching sweatshirts and the best smelling mosquito repellent made.

4kicks: 0 de skunk. That should repel even the biggest spider.

skywriter: Spend the night here Friday night 2 plan? Also get ready for pajama day, don't 4get.

lafrida: OK.

Kgirl: Good idea.

4kicks: Agree.

flikchic: I think I can.

skywriter: Done deal. Over and out.

❁

CHAPTER 2

☙

THE ANNOUNCEMENT

THE BSG had to wait until lunch to hear the formal announcement about the trip. Meanwhile, Avery was staring intently at Charlotte's yellow macaroni and cheese, orange carrots, green beans, and dish of red raspberries and blueberries mixed together.

"Avery, you can eat your super-healthy organic sprouts and turkey. I like my cafeteria food. It's a good mix. Besides," Charlotte smiled at her health-conscious friend, "I love the color combinations. They're so lively."

Katani interrupted them. "We have gym today. Do you think I could get excused? I have so much work to do."

"Nice try, Katani," said Avery. "You know the rules. You have to go to gym."

Everyone expected Katani to be as athletic as her two older sisters, but the truth was, she wasn't. In fact, she hated the whole sports competition thing. Charlotte felt bad for Katani. Having gym teachers automatically expect you to be just like your super-talented, athletic sisters would be so frustrating. As if every child in a family is a clone of the first.

Of course, Charlotte really didn't know what having siblings felt like. She was an only child, which had its good points—like never having to share a bedroom. But sometimes it was lonely. That was why being part of the BSG meant so much to her.

"Look! Here comes Mrs. Fields." Maeve nodded her head toward the principal, who had just entered the cafeteria to make an announcement.

Mrs. Fields looked elegant in a rust-colored suit with a pale yellow blouse. Charlotte knew from personal experience that the woman who kept Abigail Adams running smoothly was a wonderful grandmother to Katani. She was as much at home in the kitchen baking apple crisp as she was in the school office. Plus, she was a caring principal who was more mother than teacher when a student needed help. Charlotte remembered how kind Mrs. Fields had been to her that first day when she had made such a complete fool of herself in front of the whole school.

"This announcement is for all seventh graders ... and I can see that some of you are already on the edge of your seats in anticipation," she added wryly.

"She must be looking at Avery and Charlotte," Maeve whispered to Katani.

"She's frowning at you; you better pay attention," Katani whispered back.

"In two weeks, the seventh grade will be going on the annual outdoor education trip. The details and your supply lists will be in *The Sentinel*, as well as sent home to your parents. I do want you to know, however, that the trip is not just about having fun, which I hope you will have. This trip is designed to give you the opportunity to experience new challenges and to encourage you to work in teams ... under

✿

... *interesting* conditions."

"*Challenges*? Why doesn't she just say fighting off bears and snakes and bugs and killer mosquitoes?" Pushing away her lunch, Maeve looked pale and sick to her stomach. Charlotte didn't know whether to worry about Maeve or just laugh at her.

As soon as Mrs. Fields left the cafeteria, the buzz began.

"I heard we might have canoe races." Avery took a big bite of her turkey sandwich. Suddenly, a stream of green slime oozed onto her sleeve. "That's so gross, Avery," snapped Maeve as she put her head into her hands.

"Sooorry. I think the avocado was a little overripe." Avery wiped her sleeve off with her napkin. Charlotte marveled at Avery's nonchalance. Nothing phased that girl ... not even green avocado slime.

"Both my sisters bought hiking boots for this trip." Katani leaned on her fist. "But neither of them ever wore them again. The Summers girls aren't too keen on the big outdoors."

"This trip sounds kind of expensive." Isabel sounded worried. "What size are your sisters' boots?"

Charlotte empathized with Isabel, whose mother's treatment for multiple sclerosis sometimes made it difficult to afford everything.

Dillon Johnson, Henry Yurt, and Nick Montoya stopped at the BSG table on their way to return their trays. Nick caught Charlotte looking at him and smiled. Suddenly, the macaroni and cheese flip-flopped in her stomach. Nick really was so cute.

"Is anyone afraid of ghosts?" Dillon Johnson asked mildly, like the idea of a ghost didn't bother him at all. "My brother says there's a ghost that makes the camp his hangout."

Maeve looked up at Dillon. "Are you offering to protect

us from all the evil, nasty spirits that rise up from the deep, murky, fog-covered lagoon?"

"Uh-oh. Here we go again." Katani rolled her eyes. "What ancient horror movie is that from?" she asked.

"It's from my own personal private collection—the Maeve Kaplan-Taylor collection of horror movies that will scare the pants off of you," Maeve answered haughtily as she flipped her red curls over her shoulder.

"Whatever—ghosts, bears, mountain lions. Us he-men will be there to protect any scared-out-of-their-wits girls," pronounced Henry Yurt. Affectionately called the Yurtmeister by most of his classmates, Henry flexed his nonexistent arm muscle.

Avery made a face. "We'll see who needs help first, Yurt. I can't exactly see you winning any rope climbing contests, Mr. President."

Charlotte didn't need a crystal ball to see that working in teams with the boys was going to be a real challenge. Boys could be so incredibly ridiculous about how strong they were.

"Too bad Mrs. Fields didn't remind everyone about Pajama Day being the Friday before we leave on the trip," said Henry. Pajama Day was one of his favorite campaign promises and, to everyone's surprise, the Yurtmeister had managed to secure permission from Mrs. Fields for it to happen.

"Do you have Buzz Lightyear pjs, Yurt?" Katani smiled.

"No, teddy bears," Henry answered with true Yurt aplomb.

Isabel tugged at Katani's arm. "Let's go see if we can trade library for art, Katani. I feel an idea coming on."

"Can I come with you?" Maeve asked.

Charlotte picked up her tray. "Isabel, how about your cartoon?"

"I'm working on it. Hope you'll like it."

"I know I will." Charlotte hurried to *The Sentinel* office to do some more work on her article. The trip and supply list weren't any trouble, but she did want to add a couple of sentences to her feature article.

☞

All five BSG skidded into science class just before the last bell rang.

Ms. Weston, the new student teacher, frowned at them, but Charlotte didn't think she could look fierce if she tried. The teacher was petite, with blond hair and such electric blue eyes that Charlotte wondered if she wore contacts.

Maeve thought Ms. Weston should be singing lead in a band rather than standing in front of a room full of obnoxious seventh graders who were wondering what tricks they could play on her. Isabel and Katani thought she was a really cool dresser because one day, Ms. Weston came to school wearing a peasant skirt, cowboy boots, and a really pretty silk shirt.

"Looks can be deceiving" was more than a cliché when Ms. Weston spoke. She really knew her science, and had a way of commanding the attention of the whole class. Today she had done her homework on the class trip. "New Hampshire is a fascinating state. Did you know that its residents cast the decisive vote in ratifying the constitution? Also, the first presidential primary is held there each election year, at midnight in Dixville Notch."

"Do we get to vote on whether or not to go there?" Sammy quipped.

"You do not." Ms. Weston smiled. "The state is known as one of our great outdoor states. There are dozens of lakes and forests, some of which are filled with hiking trails that go all the way to the summits of the White Mountains."

"Can we take cameras?" Chelsea Briggs surprised everyone with her question. Usually dressed in a baggy Patriots sweatshirt, and always sitting in the back of the room, Chelsea hardly ever spoke up in class. Some of the kids still called her Chelsea Bigg, a nickname from third grade. However, Ms. R recently gave a boy detention when she overheard him say it. Mostly, kids just tended to ignore her. It was almost as if she were invisible—which was odd, because Chelsea was so large. Charlotte wondered how she felt sitting in the back of the class all the time … quiet and alone.

"Certainly, Chelsea. I know a camera is on the supply list as 'nice to have.'" Ms. Weston paused for more questions.

"I read that the New Hampshire state motto is 'Live free or die,'" Betsy Fitzgerald interjected. The class rolled their eyes. Leave it to Betsy to have already read up on New Hampshire. She could probably be giving this lecture.

"I really don't like mentioning the word 'die' along with camping and climbing mountains," Maeve said.

"Well, you may not have that much freedom on the trip either," Ms. Weston said. "But that motto also has to do with New Hampshire's history. Maybe you students would like to know that New Hampshire was the first state to have a female governor, senate president, and house speaker all at the same time."

Avery shot her fist into the air. "Oh, yeah! Just my kind of state. Sounds like New Hampshire has really enlightened voters!"

Ms. Weston smiled. Avery was one of the outspoken students and she enjoyed the energetic twelve-year-old's opinions. "I could stand here and talk all day, but instead, I've found a really great movie for you to see about the state."

✿

"Movie time. Oh, yeah!" Dillon clapped really loudly. Ms. Weston was turning out to be one of the best student teachers at Abigail Adams. She never let the class get boring.

"And you, Mr. Johnson, have the privilege of sitting by me for the whole film. Did you bring popcorn?"

Everyone laughed and jabbed at Dillon as they lined up to head to the auditorium. Maeve made sure she was beside him in line. Dillon had forgiven Maeve for a disastrous date they'd had, but for some reason, he hadn't asked for another. If Charlotte could think of one reason for Maeve to change her mind about the trip, it would be the promise of spending the week with Dillon. Although recently, Maeve had also become good friends with Riley. The musician of the class, Riley had started his own rock band with some other seventh graders, and Maeve sometimes joined them as lead singer. Maeve had told the BSG that she and Riley had a lot in common, even if Riley was a little too serious sometimes.

"He likes to talk about life and stuff," she had explained to Charlotte.

"What's wrong with that?" Charlotte wanted to know.

"Well, nothing really, I guess," Maeve had answered. "It's just that I am too busy to talk about my life. I'd rather dance," she laughed, executing a perfect dance move. Avery had tried to mimic her but failed so completely that all the BSG cracked up.

After walking down the hall for a few minutes, Charlotte looked at Isabel and giggled. They seemed to be walking in circles.

The class got quieter and quieter. Even Dillon said nothing. Nick shrugged his shoulders at Charlotte, but kept his mouth shut. The Yurtmeister just shook his head.

Finally, after they'd passed the cafeteria for the second

time, Charlotte could see a puzzled look on Ms. Weston's face. Then Katani, Ms. Take Charge, took pity on the student teacher.

"Ms. Weston," she whispered, "Do you plan to lead any of the hikes at the camp?"

"I don't know. Why do you ask?"

"Well, for one thing, we're in the wrong wing for the auditorium. Would you like me to show you where it is?"

Ms. Weston took a deep breath, her face suddenly matching her pink suede top. "I'd appreciate that, Katani. I was just beginning to realize I'd gotten turned around. I'm not the best with directions. Especially when I'm new to a place."

Turned around? Avery turned to the rest of the BSG and mouthed the word: *LOST*!

Katani took the lead and marched the class back to the auditorium. As everyone settled into their seats, Avery whispered, "I hope I'm not on Weston's team. She might be a science whiz, but she is seriously directionally challenged."

"We'll end up deep in the dark woods and have to sleep on the ground until morning." Charlotte giggled.

"Maybe on some deserted island where we can practice our survivor skills," said Nick as he slid in beside Charlotte to watch the movie. Even though they had never been on a real date, Charlotte sometimes wondered what it would be like to go out with him. She thought that being stranded on a deserted island with Nick Montoya might be fun.

Charlotte Ramsey, she scolded herself, *come back to earth right this minute!*

The travel movie made New Hampshire look as beautiful and fascinating as any place Charlotte had ever been, and that took some doing since she had seen some pretty exciting places. She wondered whether each of the fifty states in the United States had such beautiful scenery. Maybe she could set a goal of exploring every state in her lifetime.

Charlotte dreamed of becoming a writer, maybe even a travel writer, like her dad. But she sometimes wondered whether there would be room in travel books for characters who did klutzy or unexpected things. What if she went to Zambia and offended a king or something, wondered Charlotte. But then she thought about Ms. Weston, who was kind of klutzy in her own way. Maybe Charlotte could set a goal of writing a book about each state. Fifty books! She wondered, could she ever in a million years write fifty books?

Nick poked her arm. Everyone was standing. Charlotte jumped up, and in a single graceful move, managed to spill her books all over the floor and bump heads with Nick as they both bent to pick up her books. Charlotte closed her eyes and groaned.

Score another point for "Charlotte the Klutz." The only book she had any chance of writing was *Fifty Ways to Make a Fool of Yourself in Front of a Guy You Like*.

CHAPTER 3

ᘓ

FITNESS TRAINING

NO ONE got out of gym class at Abigail Adams Junior High School ... ever. "It's because of some kind of ancient rule made up by some mean principal, who said 'gym class could never be missed, even if you were dying of smallpox and you had a broken foot,'" said Maeve.

Betsy Fitzgerald overheard them. "Actually, it was President John F. Kennedy who made gym classes mandatory," she pronounced in a very official voice. "Gym is supposed to help keep kids healthy."

"Oh," shrugged Maeve. She wasn't going to argue with Betsy. Most people didn't. Betsy knew too much.

The BSG were quiet as they changed clothes in the locker room.

As she bent to tie her shoes, Charlotte announced, "My goal for the next hour is not to make a fool of myself in front of the whole class."

"I wish the whole world was watching." Avery tugged on her cross trainers. "Maybe I'd get an offer to play on a world class soccer team, or at least a scholarship to play in college."

❀

"Maybe I'll get an offer to play a role like the *Perils of Pauline*." Maeve sighed.

"*Perils of Pauline*?" Katani said, her hands on her hips. "That's a new one to me."

Maeve reminded them of the silent movie film classic at the Movie House. "Pauline was always tied to the railroad tracks and some handsome guy had to rescue her."

"Oh, oh, save me please. I'm just a helpless girl." Avery waved her hands back and forth in front of her face and squeaked out her plea for help. "How pathetic."

Maeve, being Maeve, refused to take offense and instead pumped up her arms and lowered her voice. "I will save you if you are the wealthy heir to the Madden fortune, and you will promise to marry me and sign over all your rights to the money. But if you're not, forget it."

Pushing and giggling, they stumbled into the gym. Coach McCarthy clapped his hands immediately. "All right, campers in training, start with a warmup mile around the gym. I'll time you. Pick up the pace, Kaplan-Taylor." Maeve could dance for hours, but running was not her thing. "Most dancers," her instructor told her, "save their knees for the dance." The truth was, Maeve just didn't like to run.

"Just wait until you're a famous actress in Hollywood, Maeve," Avery whispered. She held up a make-believe microphone. "I'd like to thank my junior high gym teacher for making me angry enough to succeed." Avery took off jogging, catching up to Charlotte.

"Why does he keep picking on her?" Charlotte whispered. "Just because she isn't a fast runner ... I think it's mean. He doesn't even care that she is probably the best dancer in the school."

Nick jogged up behind them. "Race you, Madden."

"Beating you isn't satisfying enough. I'm saving myself for a higher goal in life, Montoya." Avery left Nick jogging beside Charlotte. Charlotte couldn't talk and run really fast at the same time. But it was great having Nick beside her to help her keep up her pace.

Katani was turning out to be a pretty decent runner. She was running just behind the Trentini twins by the end of the mile.

The BSG caught their breath while Maeve finished her last lap. She had started out OK, but kept falling behind. "You know, Coach McCarthy, this would be so much more fun if we had music. And I think we'd train better, don't you?" She flashed him a megawatt smile, hoping her enthusiasm would encourage him to agree.

"Yeah, music. Sure. OK, Kaplan. Go find some." Suddenly, everyone had suggestions. Billy Trentini voted for reggae. Yurt wanted Aerosmith. "Some sixties rock and roll," Riley Lee suggested. "It's got a good beat for running. I'll go to the music room. I know just what we need. I'll be back before you all can say New Hampshire." Billy Trentini rolled his eyes at Riley's awkward attempt at humor. Musical—Riley was. Funny—he wasn't.

Riley took off before Mr. McCarthy could say no. The coach shrugged and handed out jump ropes.

Charlotte groaned. She could jog, but if there was anything to trip her up, jump roping was it. It required a rhythm she hadn't quite mastered yet. She'd be down more often than not. "Let's do some double dutch," she suggested. "I'll turn one end."

"I'll get the other." Katani grabbed the ends of two long ropes. She and Charlotte started swinging. The ropes hit the floor in a beat that made Katani tap her foot. Maybe she wasn't athletic, but Katani got the tapping down. Charlotte tried the tapping, but she felt like a dork. She couldn't seem to coordinate her arms and her feet at the same time. The whole thing was a jumble. It's a good thing I can kick a soccer ball, sighed Charlotte.

True to his promise, Riley was back and had a disc in the CD player in minutes.

When "La Bamba" came blasting through the gym, Charlotte wasn't surprised. She'd just edited Riley's column for the newspaper. He'd written about Ritchie Valens, one of the first Hispanic rock and rollers, and his short, tragic life.

Riley was an interesting person, Isabel thought. He likes to experiment just like me. Maybe that's the way artists are.

Even though most of the kids didn't know who Ritchie Valens was, everyone picked up the pace to match the music. Charlotte was swinging ropes, dancing in place, actually having fun, and when it came time for her to jump, the music seemed to help. She actually made it through her turn without tripping—a first. She felt elated.

"OK, ropes away," Mr. McCarthy shouted. "Up the bleacher stairs, across the top, back down the other side. Three times. Go, go, go!"

Maeve glanced over at Isabel and Katani. Running up and down the bleachers was not anyone's idea of a good time, except for a few die-hard athletes like Avery. Maeve wished they could go jump over the hurdles. That was fun. Even eager beaver Betsy Fitzgerald didn't look happy about the stairs.

Avery and Billy Trentini took off like they were being chased by wild dogs. Bolting up the stairs two at a time, the two of them reached the top simultaneously and were on their way down before Maeve was even on the third step. Music or no music, sighed Maeve, this was going to be one long gym period. She would just have to think of other things like dancing in a beautiful ball gown under the stars with a famous movie star. That was more like it, she fantasized, and was surprised to find herself suddenly on the way down.

Next, Coach McCarthy organized sprints. How Avery had energy left after the stairs was more than Charlotte could fathom. Everyone else, except for Billy Trentini, was panting for air. And sprints were killer races. You had to bolt like a racehorse and run as fast as you could 'til it felt like your lungs were exploding. It seemed to Maeve that the coach was trying to kill them before they even left on the trip. He assured them that this was getting them in shape, but it seemed more like getting ready for Marine boot camp.

Maeve thought it was really strange that she could dance for a couple hours, sweat like a popsicle in the sun, and not be out of breath. Yet, running a sprint made her feel like her lungs were burning up. She guessed it was like her dad always said, "Different strokes for different folks."

"I almost beat both Nick and Dillon," Katani said. "Can you believe that? Can they believe that?" She laughed while sucking in great quantities of air.

"It's those long legs of yours, Katani," huffed Isabel. "You should take up running. You're pretty good."

"No way, Isabel," Katani admonished in a mock serious tone, but inside she was thinking, this running isn't too bad.

"Is class over? This is the longest fifty minutes of my life," Maeve complained. Suddenly, the music went off.

"I've saved just enough time for the rope climb." Coach McCarthy grinned, looking rather pleased with himself. "Half of you," the coach divided the class with a swing of his hand, "climb those ropes to the top, ring the bell, and come down. No rope burns, please. The other half, to the wall. Kaplan, you're first."

Charlotte really thought the coach was over-the-top hard on Maeve today. She squeezed Maeve's arm in a show of support. "You'll make it, Maeve."

Half of one wall in the gym was covered with a grid of ropes. You needed to be a spider to climb them clear to the top of the gym. If you were afraid of heights, the climb was hard. Maeve was nervous and she didn't like heights. But she didn't want anyone thinking she was wimpy, so she put on her "I'm not afraid of anything" face, and started climbing.

Charlotte had never quite made it all the way to the top. Would Maeve be able to do it? she questioned.

"Yurt, you and Johnson spot. Montoya, pull over the mats."

"Coach, we always have four people spotting. And a fifth spotter who doesn't take their eyes off the climber the whole time. When did you change the rules?" Katani spoke up for Maeve. She wondered if she should speak to her grandmother about Coach McCarthy. He wasn't being very careful, she thought.

Coach didn't answer the question, but he sent Betsy, Billy, and Nick over to join the spotters.

Maeve flashed Katani a grateful look from the fifth rung up. She looked graceful at first, her long red hair in a ponytail, legs and arms reaching, pulling. But her fists were white, grasping the rope, hanging on for dear life.

She was maybe ten, twelve rungs up the wall when her foot slipped. Her hair came loose, and she couldn't see. In seconds she was hanging from her hands and scrambling to get her footing. Her feet were flailing in the air, trying to find a place to land. Then she smashed her knee into the wall.

Her scream, right out of the old movies, echoed off the walls and wooden floor, and in one instant stopped all activity in the gym.

All the BSG gasped and stood up. Katani grabbed Charlotte's arm. "She's really freaked."

"Someone do something." Isabel bit her lip.

Coach McCarthy headed for the ropes. But Dillon and the student teacher who had just entered the gym, Ms. Meadows, were there first. They climbed like spiders, hand over hand, legs following, until they reached Maeve.

Dillon stabilized the bottom rung so Maeve could get her foot back in. At the same time Ms. Meadows spoke softly to Maeve, encouraging her to breathe deeply and reach for the rope with her right hand.

All eyes were on Maeve as she struggled to regain her control of the ropes. Finally, with a little help from Ms. Meadows, Maeve regained her grip and gingerly made her way down. When she hit the ground she looked as if she would faint.

The gym was silent until Coach McCarthy directed everyone back to their activities.

"Good show, Dillon." Avery patted Dillon on the back. "You're a real hero, that was such a good move; you were really fast ..." Avery talked too much when she was scared, and Maeve had scared them all.

Maeve's face was still pale, and she wouldn't loosen her grip on the ropes, even though she was now on the ground. She was also clearly embarrassed. Pink spots were beginning to appear on her face.

Charlotte moved to one side of her, Katani to the other. "We're going to the locker room, Mr. McCarthy." Charlotte dared him to say no. She was so furious at the thought of a

❀

teacher making a student do something they weren't ready for, that Charlotte spoke with a courage that she hadn't realized she possessed. But this was Maeve ... her friend. Somehow it felt easier sticking up for a friend than for yourself. But Maeve wouldn't look at any of the BSG and ran right for the locker room.

Avery, Charlotte, Isabel, and Katani stared at Mr. McCarthy until his face was almost as white as Maeve's. As he shooed them out with both hands, Isabel noticed that his hands were shaking.

In the locker room, all the BSG crowded around Maeve as she iced her knee.

"You showed him, Maeve," Avery enthused. "Maybe McCarthy won't pick on you so much any more."

"Yeah, I think he felt bad." Isabel looked wrung out, as if she'd just run a marathon.

"I bet he was thinking he was going to get fired," Katani piped in, her voice thick with anger.

"Dillon's the Spider Man of the seventh grade." Charlotte laughed. "It was so, so ... romantic." She hoped Maeve would appreciate that.

Maeve suddenly exploded. "I totally nearly fell. My knee really hurts and I feel like a total idiot," she shouted and leaned forward, burying her face in her hands.

The rest of the BSG stared at each other. They knew Maeve's near fall had been frightening for her, but they didn't know how to react.

Avery leaned over and gave Maeve a little pat on the shoulder. For Avery, that was tantamount to giving someone a bear hug. Maeve looked up at her with a half smile.

A very quiet huddle of Beacon Street Girls changed out of their gym uniforms. No one was coming in to check on them and all of the other girls had gone, so there was no one left to gossip about Maeve's mini-breakdown.

Maeve looked sheepishly at her friends, wiping her face with her towel. "Sorry, guys. I didn't mean to shout at you. But I really felt like I was going to fall and when I couldn't find the rungs, I was so scared. I'm just not good at those ropes."

"It's OK, Maeve," Charlotte whispered. "Nobody's good at everything. Have you seen Avery dance?" Maeve started to giggle. "I say we all walk to Montoya's ... grab some hot chocolate. My treat," offered Charlotte.

The last bell rang. Relieved, they all gathered up their backpacks, heading for their lockers and over to Beacon Street and their favorite bakery.

On the way, the girls grumbled about how unfair Coach McCarthy was. Katani really thought she should tell her grandmother. But Maeve completely forbade her.

"That's all I need. He'll think I'm a tattletale and he'll be mad for the rest of my junior high career."

None of the other BSG could convince Maeve that Katani was right.

ભ

"Chelsea, is that you? What are you doing in here? Why weren't you in class?" Valerie Meadows was frowning as she sat down beside Chelsea on a bench that was almost hidden in the back corner of the locker room.

Chelsea Briggs had been hiding in the back of the room for the whole period. It was no big deal. She had done it before. Mr. McCarthy hardly ever took roll, and of course, he never looked into the girls' locker room. But today ... Chelsea was unlucky. How was she supposed to know the new student teacher for gym would come in and snoop around.

"How do you know my name?" Chelsea asked, avoiding the question.

"I plan to teach gym and coach girls' basketball next year at Abigail Adams—I hope. So I tried to learn all the students' names."

"You aren't tall enough to play basketball." Chelsea had only glanced at Ms. Meadows, but she wasn't that tall. Basketball players needed to be tall.

"That's what the coach said when I came into ninth grade and went out for the team. I proved him wrong. Sometimes doing something well depends on attitude rather than size."

Size. Ms. Meadows had probably been wondering how she could introduce that word into the conversation, and Chelsea had just given her the perfect opportunity.

"So why are you here ... have you been crying?" she inquired sympathetically.

"NO," Chelsea answered a little too loudly. "I just hate gym. My doctor says I am supposed to lose thirty pounds—he said something about Type 2 diabetes. Whatever."

Chelsea couldn't believe that she blurted that out to a total stranger. The gym teacher could see that she needed to lose thirty pounds. Everyone could see Chelsea was "weight challenged." Why did she have to broadcast it? At least no kids were around to hear how much weight she was supposed to lose, a relieved Chelsea thought. Then she looked up and added for good measure, "And Mr. McCarthy hates me."

"I don't think that is true, Chelsea. I think he only expects you to do your best, to at least try to participate," the perky student teacher admonished. "Are there any games that you like in gym? How about volleyball?"

Chelsea raised one eyebrow. "I think I'll pass on the volleyball. I'm not wild about the uniform, if you know what

I mean."

The student teacher bit her lip to keep from smiling. "I don't know, Chelsea. You might like it. Lots of kids who hate other sports have fun with volleyball."

Chelsea just shrugged her shoulders, and then … *trouble*. Ms. Meadows asked for her note from home.

Chelsea had begged and pleaded with her mother to please ask her pediatrician to give her a note so she wouldn't have to take gym, but all her mother had said was, "You need the exercise."

"Mom," Chelsea had shouted. "Mr. McCarthy yells at me if I walk instead of jog. I hate to jog. And everyone looks at me funny. Why is everyone so obsessed about exercise anyway? I'd rather watch TV."

Now Ms. Meadows was probably thinking the same thing as her mother. Gym teachers were so full of themselves, thought Chelsea somewhat angrily.

"I'm sorry, Chelsea, but I'm going to have to ask you to go talk to Mrs. Fields before you go home," said Ms. Meadows.

"Go to the principal's office? Just because I sat out gym class?"

Chelsea had never ever been sent to the principal's office before. This was not good. In fact, things were getting grim. Mrs. Fields would call her mother (and she'd go home and get another lecture). Then her mother would make some low-cal boring dinner and tell Chelsea to take a bike ride. Yeah, that'd work, sighed Chelsea. Every time she did any walking or riding on the stationary bike (as if she was going to ride around the neighborhood all by herself), the activity only made her hungry, and eating seemed like the perfect reward for carrying out her mother's wishes.

Reluctantly, Chelsea took the pink slip Ms. Meadows

handed her and bit her lip as she headed down the hall.

At least maybe everyone would have gone home and wouldn't see her reporting to Mrs. Fields' office.

Whew! Luck was now on her side. The school secretary had gone home. Now, just maybe Mrs. Fields wouldn't be there either ...

Ruby Fields, cup of coffee in hand, walked up behind Chelsea.

"Chelsea, are you looking for me?"

How could Mrs. Fields remember every kid's name in the entire school? Of course, Chelsea figured once anyone saw her, how could they forget "the big girl"? The boys used to tease her in elementary school a lot, but she had mastered the art of ignoring the junior high male. The occasional complete jerk still got to her every once in a while. But the girls ... they were harder to ignore. The girls weren't outright mean, but Chelsea knew they always talked about her behind her back. She had seen the looks, the whispering, and the pointing. And it had hurt ... sometimes really badly.

Junior high was better than elementary school, even though it was lonely. Kids pretty much left her alone. The maturity thing, Chelsea thought without enthusiasm.

"Yes, ma'am."

"Come into my office, and close the door behind you. I'm sure everyone but the custodian has gone home, but we'll have some privacy. What's the problem?"

Chelsea handed Mrs. Fields the pink slip, figuring she might as well get right to the point.

"I skipped gym. The new student teacher caught me. I tried to tell her that I had permission to sit out today, but—"

"And do you have a note to miss gym? From your mother? May I see it, please?"

Chelsea should have known Mrs. Fields was too smart for that lame excuse to work. "Well, I couldn't find it. I guess—"

"Don't you have an older brother, Chelsea? Seems like I remember him from a couple of years ago."

"Yes. Ben. Big Ben."

"He plays football at the high school, doesn't he? Linebacker?"

"He's a tackle. No one can get past him," Chelsea said proudly. *Because* he's so huge, Chelsea added to herself. It was all right to be huge if you wanted to fall on people and stop them from getting to your quarterback. She wondered if Mrs. Fields was going to ask her if she had plans to play football someday. "I've never been good at sports."

"Why not?" Mrs Fields smiled, swung her chair around, opened a small fridge, and pulled out a bottle of water. She handed it to Chelsea without asking if she wanted it.

Chelsea's throat felt as dry as the Sahara Desert. She opened the bottle and took a big swallow before she answered. "Thank you. I guess I was really thirsty. It's not that I'm not good. I'm too slow." Chelsea didn't want to mention the weight word. Let Mrs. Fields figure that one out for herself.

"It's hard always coming in last, or dropping the ball, or—"

"Yeah. It is," Chelsea admitted.

"Do they laugh, or are you afraid they will?"

"Some of them laugh. They try to hide it sometimes, but they laugh."

"What are you good at?"

Chelsea looked up at the principal. Mrs. Fields seemed to want to know. What the heck, thought Chelsea.

"Taking pictures. I'm a pretty good photographer. Sometimes I take pictures at parties in my neighborhood.

You know, little kids' parties, and pets. People's pets. I get paid. Twenty dollars. That's not much, but I like doing it," she said emphatically.

Mrs. Fields rocked her office chair back and forth for a minute. Probably thinking up what punishment Chelsea should have. Double gym periods for a month, probably.

"Would you bring some photos in to show me? Your favorites, or a photo album if you have one. You should make a book of your best photos to show people when you're trying to get jobs."

Chelsea took a slow sip of water and looked at Mrs. Fields. The principal seemed sincere … interested in seeing some photos. But teachers and principals were supposed to be sincere. They kind of got paid for that. But Mrs. Fields was smiling at her. So maybe she really meant what she said.

"OK. I can do that."

Mrs. Fields stood up, suggesting that the meeting was over. No detention, no running laps (Coach McCarthy's favorite punishment), no calling her mom.

Chelsea hurried to escape before Mrs. Fields could figure out some heinous thing for her to do to make up for skipping class. "Thanks. I'll stop by on a free period or after lunch someday."

Just before she walked out the door Mrs. Fields called to her. Shoot. Chelsea clenched her fists. I'm busted.

"Chelsea, I expect to see you in gym class from now on. And for your information, Chelsea, we don't tolerate name-calling or bullying in this school. If you are ever uncomfortable here, I want to hear about it."

Chelsea nodded. She would never be able to skip gym again. Everyone would be on the lookout now for Chelsea Briggs for sure. She'd have to go to gym for the rest of her junior high existence. And the name-calling. She'd have to think about that.

By the time Chelsea got outside, she had missed the bus. She fished her cell phone out of her backpack and called her mother to tell her that she was walking home. She didn't live that far, and walking would give her time to think. Her mom felt safe letting Chelsea walk down Harvard and onto Beacon. The street was busy, the neighborhood friendly and safe, and all the shop owners, especially Yuri, who owned the fruit store, kept an eye out for the Abigail Adams students.

∽

Chelsea Briggs'
PERSONAL, SUPER-PRIVATE JOURNAL
NO TRESPASSING ...Ever!

I can't believe Mrs. Fields didn't punish me big time for skipping gym. I figured a detention at least. But she didn't even talk about it that much. She wanted to know more about me ... what I liked. Nice principal!

Tomorrow I'm going to take Mrs. Fields some of my pictures. I think she meant it when she asked to see some.

BTW—there is no way I want to go on this camping trip. Does "dread" ring a bell? Maybe I can get out of it somehow. The rules say we'll have teams. Like anyone would want me on their team.

I don't even really have a friend. If it's like those survivor programs, I'll get picked to go home first. But what if I don't? What if I stick it out, swim every day, climb palm trees, and eat only coconuts and fish, and lose about a hundred pounds? I'll get home and no one will know me. I can change schools and start over as the skinny girl with the tan. And besides, I'll be famous, have a million dollars, and no one would ever give me weird looks again. Only one problem—I hate coconuts and I can't climb trees—guess the "stuck on an island" thing is out.

I kind of like Charlotte Ramsey. We could be friends maybe, if I ever talked to her while I'm at The Sentinel office. But she has so many friends, why would she need me for a friend?

She was brand new at school this year and shazam, just like that, she ended up with four friends. They call themselves the Beacon Street Girls. I guess it's a club they have, although they don't call it a club.

I'm going to start my own magazine called "Leave Me ALONE." Regular features to include:

- *No fat talk—ever*
- *Boys are not the most important people in our lives*
- *Eat—you'll live longer*
- *Cool clothes for every size and shape*
- *Name-callers need to get a life*
- *Exercise—forgetaboutit—try fun instead*
- *TV is interesting*

Signed:

Chelsea Briggs (photographer to the Stars)
World Famous Pet Photographer ☆ Friend of the Rich and Famous
(stranger things have happened)

Chelsea closed her journal and sighed. It was easy to write about changing your life. But doing it was much, much harder.

CHAPTER 4

❧

MIXED NUTS

AVERY—THERE ARE NO GHOSTS!

AVERY YAWNED as she gathered her tangled black hair into a ponytail and secured it with her lucky hair tie—the one with purple soccer balls all over it. As always, her hair seemed to be going in all directions, but Avery couldn't care less. When she sat down at the kitchen counter for breakfast, she wondered if a little brother like Maeve's would be as much a pain in the you-know-what as a big brother. Specifically, Scott.

"Lake Rescue, hey, that's a great place to go." Scott looked into three boxes of cereal before he found one to suit him, or that wasn't almost empty. Mrs. Madden wasn't the type of mother who got up and made bacon, eggs, and waffles every morning. That was actually a good thing because Avery and Scott liked cereal anyway.

"You know, Ave, there's really a ghost at the camp. I don't think anyone knows who it is, but one theory is that it's a seventh-grade camper left behind who starved to death before he could find his way home."

"You don't scare me, Scott. I don't believe that for a minute," Avery retorted as she took a bite of granola. "I'm sure there are phones at the camp, and almost everyone has a cell these days. Why didn't he just call someone to come and get him, duh?"

"Duh, not in 1957, Ave. That camp is really old. Half the buildings are falling down. I'll bet a bunch of them are haunted. But this ghost I'm talking about is the one everyone is afraid of."

"How come?" Avery glanced over and carefully studied all the strange boxes and vegetables piled near the sink. Was her mother experimenting again tonight for dinner? Typically, if her mother wanted to entertain, she hired a caterer to bring the food.

Avery hoped she wasn't still on her "let's introduce Avery to every authentic Asian dish known to mankind" kick. Since she had been adopted as a baby, Avery figured her "ethnic palate" was Gerber's baby food, strained peas, applesauce, chocolate pudding, stuff like that. Although, Avery did like bulkogi—it was her favorite Korean beef dish of all time. And, she had to admit that experimenting with new foods kept things interesting. One time her mother even brought them to an Ethiopian restaurant. Avery remembered how much fun she and Katani and Scott had had, scooping up all the tasty food with this really chewy bread. It had been so cool to eat with their hands instead of forks.

"Are you listening, Ave?" Scott kept on. "This ghost is real, believe me. One night I woke up to someone screaming and then a moaning sound. And then some creepy voice was crying, 'Bring it back, bring it back.'"

"Yeah, I remember that story. 'Bring back my head.' I heard it that time Mom sent me to that awesome Girl Scout camp. Everyone who has ever been to camp knows the story. And, I don't believe in ghosts, Scott."

"I don't know, Ave. I think you should think ..."

Avery watched Scott drink the leftover milk from his cereal bowl, put on his coat, and scoot out the kitchen door. "Later, Ave," he called over his shoulder.

"Get pepperoni pizza tonight," she yelled after him.

There couldn't really be a ghost at this camp, could there? Avery sat sipping her tea, shivering despite the warm liquid. She tried to think only about hiking, climbing, and canoeing ... not spooky apparitions wandering the paths at night. A lot of people believed that if you died when you were unhappy, your spirit might hang around for awhile. Avery had heard some kids complain because they had to go to Lake Rescue. She wondered if it was because they had heard about the ghosts.

Avery gathered her books and made sure she had her homework. As she walked past the hall closet to the front door, she heard a thump and then a rustling. The hairs on the back of her neck stood up and her heart began to pound. Suddenly, the door burst open. Avery screamed at the top of her lungs and jumped back. She threw her bag at a tall, hooded figure.

"Oww! Avery. That thing hurts." Scott pushed back the hood of his sweatshirt and rubbed his head.

"That's not funny, Scott. You could have given me a heart attack," Avery shouted at her brother.

"It was a joke. I feel sorry for the ghost if he runs into you."

"What's going on here?" Avery's mom asked as she walked down the stairs, a pile of clothing in her arms.

"Nothing, Mom," Scott and Avery replied in their best angelic voices.

"For the ten hundredth time, Mom, I don't want to go to that camp. Can't you please, *please* write me an excuse? I don't mind staying in study hall or wherever they want to put the people who aren't going. I mean really, can you see me climbing a mountain or paddling a canoe?"

Maeve looked at the wrinkled shirt she was going to have to wear. It was clean, but no one had taken it out of the dryer in time. She longed for the good old days when her mother kept all her clothes perfectly ironed and folded.

"Maeve, it will be good for you to go camping. All your friends are going. You don't want to be left behind."

"Yes I do. I'll do some extra tutoring sessions. I'll catch up on every class where I'm behind. I'll even jog in the park every day. I'll write an extra paper on—on, well, on children adjusting to divorce."

"Maeve, that was uncalled for and you know it." Ms. Kaplan looked like a stylish Wall Street businesswoman. No wrinkled clothes for her. Maeve figured if her dad saw Mom today, he'd beg to come back home.

"Sorry, Mom. But you know how much I hate snakes and spiders and anything that slithers or flies around buzzing. You or Sam will have to feed Buttercup and Westley. And their cage is dirty. I could clean it if I stayed home."

"Buttercup and Westley?" Her mother looked puzzled.

"The guinea pigs, Mom. See, if you can't even remember their names …"

"Maeve, I'm sure Sam can feed those guinea pigs, whose names you change every week, and you can clean the cage before you go. There's plenty of time."

"I wish I could go," Sam said. "I could dress in my camouflage clothes and your friends could smuggle me onto the bus. Once we got to camp, they couldn't send me home." Sam was building a house out of shredded wheat biscuits.

"Sam, like no one is going to notice."

"You think your clueless friends would figure things out?"

"My friends are not clueless. Katani and Charlotte are on the honor roll, for your information."

"Maybe they can teach you how to make the honor roll."

"Samuel Kaplan-Taylor. You apologize to your sister ... right now."

Sam knew he had crossed the line. Maeve's struggles with schoolwork were off-limits in their sibling rivalry.

"I'm really, really, really, sorry, double sorry, Maeve."

Maeve threw a piece of toast at him.

"Sam, you're staying with your father when Maeve goes to camp," Maeve's mother said. "I'm going to have some time all to myself." She looked kind of dreamy-eyed.

Maeve suddenly felt uneasy. Her mother had been acting kind of strange lately. What if she wanted time to herself so she could go on dates with other men? That would be completely awful. And how would it make her dad feel? This separation stuff was for the birds.

"Maybe Sam could stay with one of his friends and you and Dad could go on a date?" Maeve almost forgot begging to get out of camp. "You'd have all weekend to talk about things. How your life was BK, you know, before kids."

"Maeve, how I spend my weekend is not your concern. Maybe I'll spend the whole weekend in bed reading and eating chocolates."

Maeve almost wished for the days when her mother planned a rigid schedule for her, found her tutors for every subject, complained if she had any fun at all.

"You're going to Lake Rescue, Maeve, and that's my final answer. Don't beg me to let you stay home again." Ms. Kaplan walked out the door, leaving Maeve to get Sam off to school and lock up.

Maeve stared at her cold oatmeal and sighed. Maybe she would have to eat spider oatmeal at Lake Rescue.

Of course, there was always the dance. What if it was the social event of the year? I guess I could deal with a few spiders, as long as they weren't too big, she reasoned.

ISABEL—BUGS AND SNAKES AND EVERYTHING NICE!

"Isabel, no self-respecting Martinez is afraid of bugs!" Elena Maria, Isabel's ninth-grade sister, loved camping. Because they had recently moved to Brookline, Elena had missed going on the outdoor program. She and her father had camped a lot around the Great Lakes and it was her favorite thing to do. She was a little envious that Isabel was going to New Hampshire, a place she had never been.

"You know very well that even the word 'spider' freaks me out. Do you remember those tarantulas in Mexico with their big hairy legs? Too bad you missed out on Lake Rescue, Elena. *Deseas venir?*"

Elena Maria laughed. "OK. I am a little jealous. You caught me. But, you can relax. There are no tarantulas in the White Mountains. I'm pretty sure of that ... why don't you just tell Mama you don't want to go?"

"I don't want to worry her, now that she's finally feeling better. Besides, I do sort of want to go. I like being outside. I just wish we could sleep in a hotel instead of cabins. And, you know, I worry about Mama too."

Since they had moved to Brookline the sisters had become very protective of their mother. They were both hoping that the famous Boston hospitals and doctors could help her MS—and they had. But living apart from Papa, even with Mama's sister, was getting expensive.

"Mama, you're looking *muy bonita* today." Isabel ran to kiss her mother and help her sit at the table.

"I'm so glad I got to the table before you left, Isabel. Tell me more about this trip your class is taking."

"It's camping and hiking and stuff like that. 'Outdoor education' they call it. But you know, Mama, getting some of the things I'm going to need, like hiking boots, is going to be expensive. I don't really mind missing it."

"Oh, I wouldn't think of letting you miss the trip. Aren't all your friends going? You'll have so much fun. Your father was able to send a little extra money this month. We'll manage. I want you to write down everything you see, all the new plants and animals."

"And such interesting bugs and snakes, spiders especially," Elena Maria said innocently. "I'm late. See you tonight." Elena hurried out the door. Sisters, Isabel sighed. They could be so sneaky.

"*Hija*, you will write about how the trees smell and describe the wild flowers. And the birds. You know how I love your birds. You'll see some new ones, I'm sure. Draw pictures of all the birds and wild flowers. Take your colored pencils. If you do that, you can share so many details, and I'll feel as if I've been on the trip with you."

There was so much longing in Mama's voice that Isabel felt ashamed. Here she was complaining about having to go on a trip just because of a few spiders, and her mother was only wishing that she could go along. Suddenly, the idea of going to Lake Rescue held promise. Maybe she could do a whole book for her mother. It would be fun. Talking with her mom had inspired her. She could see the title now: *A Little Bird Told Me.*

"Oh, I will, Mama. I will. I'll draw a picture on every page of my journal and when you see them and I tell you what I saw and did, you'll feel as if you really did go there, too."

"*Buena, mi hija.* Someday, you will be a famous artist, I just know it."

Isabel tipped up her glass of orange juice, drained it, kissed her mother good-bye, and ran out of the house. If she didn't hurry, she would be late for school. She hated racing by Mrs. Fields' office as the principal stood outside the door, tapping her watch at the kids who were late.

❀

KATANI—OLDER SISTERS ARE USELESS!

Katani was sitting at the breakfast table with both hands waving in the air. She had just painted her fingernails gold and hoped they'd dry so she could eat and get to school on time. She had laid out her clothes last night, painted her nails, then this morning had changed her mind completely. No way could she have pink nails with the orange top she'd decided to change to.

"Paint mine," her sister Kelley begged. "Gold fingernails are magic." Kelley was fourteen, two years older than Katani, but she was mildly autistic, so often acted like a much younger child.

"No time, Kelley. Tonight, I promise. Tonight we'll paint your nails and put little stickers on them."

"I want Sponge Bob stickers on my nails."

"You got it, girlfriend." Katani blew her sister an air kiss.

Her two older sisters—Candice, who was home from college for a few days, and Patrice, who was still in high school—hurried into the kitchen. Both carried an armload of clothes, shoes, backpacks, flashlights—camping gear from their seventh-grade treks into the wilderness.

Katani would have none of it. "Never mind, guys. I'm not going on this trip."

"What do you mean you're not going?" Patrice said. "You have to go. Only if you were in the hospital or broke your leg or something, could you get out of it. You're probably going to hate every minute of it—no place to do your nails—but it's a tradition. Here are the shoes I think might fit Isabel. They belonged to Candice and were too small, so I had to get new ones. I think you can wear mine. What a waste. We only wore them once, or at least I did."

"Me too. I would never have worn them to school, and I

needed dressy clothes for work." Candice looked in the fridge. "Don't tell me we're out of applesauce again."

"Who wants eggs with mushrooms and cheese?" asked Patrice, who was standing at the stove. "Don't forget it's your turn to finish loading the dishwasher, Katani. You're not getting out of it just because your nails aren't dry."

Patrice was younger than Candice, but she liked to boss the entire family around. Only when their grandmother was in the room did she keep her mouth shut. Katani couldn't help but think how Patrice could be so annoying sometimes.

Mrs. Summers rushed into the kitchen wearing her tailored black suit with a white silk blouse. "No eggs for me today, all I have time for is a yogurt and coffee. Patrice, hand me a raspberry and toss some granola in it. I spent half the night getting ready for this trial today. You each have exactly a minute apiece to present any problems you have that you can't solve yourselves." Mrs. Summers blew kisses at her daughters. She was a super lawyer who believed in instilling independence in children at an early age. "Nothing? Good. I'm leaving. Call me at work if you need me. And," she added with a wide grin, "call the FBI if you can't find me."

Kelley jumped to envelop her mother in a hug. "I am going to call the FBI, the FBI, oh me, oh my," she sang.

Candice, Patrice, and Katani all laughed. Kelley could be so funny sometimes. Their mother put her finger to her mouth, not wanting to overexcite Kelley before she left.

"Mom, wait, I do have one problem. I just don't have time to go on this outdoor education thing the school is having. I have two papers to write and I want to join the math club. Will you write me an excuse to stay at school?" asked Katani, hoping her nonchalant tone would distract her mother from the question.

❁

"Oh, the Lake Rescue trip? Is it that time already? Of course you're going. Candice and Patrice loved the experience. It's one of your grandmother's favorite school trips. You loved it, didn't you, girls?"

"We sure did." Candice smiled ever so sweetly at Katani. "No way can you miss it."

"All your friends are going," Patrice reminded Katani. "It's the experience of a lifetime, or maybe junior high time. It's a school ritual. Grandma Ruby would never let you miss it, either."

"See, Katani? Have a great day, girls. You can't reach me until afternoon. If you can't reach me or your dad, call Grandma Ruby." Mrs. Summers took a last sip of coffee, grabbed her briefcase and keys, and left nibbling on a piece of toast. She poked her head back in. "Remember, friday night, Katani. I'm taking your friends shopping, right? Maybe we can shop for the trip. Now, wish me luck."

"Luck, Mom." Katani heard her mother race out and start her car. "Thanks for all your help." Katani glared at Patrice and Candice.

"You're welcome." Both girls, smiling sweetly, rinsed their plates and forks, leaving the dishwasher open. "Bye, Kelley. Be good today."

Kelley stared at Katani when they were the only two left at the table. "You can take Mr. Bear, Katani. That way you won't be lonely for me at night."

"That's so sweet, Kel." Katani reached over and hugged her sister. Kelley never parted with Mr. Bear. The stuffed bear kept her grounded. What do I have to to complain about … really, thought Katani. Kelley was the one who had things to complain about and she never did.

Katani finished loading the dishes, then placed the hiking

boots in a grocery bag to take for Isabel to try on. She hurried Kelly out of the house to walk her to school. Maybe she could run through the woods at Lake Rescue. That might be fun.

CHAPTER 5

❦

BOOTS AND BUGS

"TGIF." Charlotte felt as if this week had been two weeks long. Getting *The Sentinel* page finished took more time than usual, but Charlotte thought this might be their best issue ever. Plus, she had helped with the layout of the seventh-grade page. She had contributed way more than just as a feature writer, and she had enjoyed it.

What if she learned enough from Jennifer that she could try out for editor next year? Did she want to be editor? Being an editor and being a writer were two very different things, but as editor she'd learn a lot about writing. Maybe it would even help her get into college someday, Charlotte dreamed. Suddenly, she stopped herself. Wow, she almost laughed out loud. I'm turning into Betsy Fitzgerald. Betsy's whole motivation in life was building her college resume even though she was only twelve. I've got to chill out here. Charlotte shrugged her shoulders.

Glancing at the newspaper, Charlotte noticed that the only thing missing today was Isabel's cartoon, but the size was standard, so they left a hole for it to slip into. Jennifer said "no problem," she was staying until everything was perfect. "It's my job," she shrugged.

When the bell rang, Charlotte ran to get her backpack so she could meet her friends on the front steps of the school. They were going "Lake Rescue shopping." Charlotte couldn't wait.

When Charlotte got to the front of the school she saw Isabel rushing toward her.

"Isabel!" Charlotte shouted to her friend. She was first at the steps. The BSG were going shopping with Katani's mother. Katani had explained that shopping for Lake Rescue was a tradition. Her mom had done this for Patrice and Candice too. Charlotte got the idea that everyone in Katani's family loved tradition. She also knew Katani felt like she was disappointing her family by not being a super athlete like her sisters. But Charlotte could tell that Mr. and Mrs. Summers were proud of all their daughters. You could see it in their faces when they looked at Katani.

"Isabel, did you turn in your cartoon?" Charlotte asked.

Isabel was breathing hard. "I was afraid I would be late." She usually looked so cool, even with a spot of paint on her clothing. The mark of a true artist. Today her long black hair was tangled and a silver clip barely hung in place. Isabel knew she looked a mess. She collapsed on the steps and searched in her purse for a hairbrush.

"I turned it in just now. I thought I'd have time to finish it during library, but then Ms. O'Reilly assigned that new report." In a couple of minutes, Isabel was back together, her hair glistening and pinned together, not a strand out of place. Her dangly silver earrings set off her long neck and glittered in the sunlight.

"How do you do that?" Charlotte asked. "If I had looked

as frazzled as you did just now, it would have taken me three mirrors and an hour to get myself together." She laughed.

"I guess when you dance in shows, you learn to change clothes and tidy up fast. The real stars even have help because they have to change costumes three or four times. But even amateur dancers like me learn to do the quick change." Isabel sighed.

"You miss your dancing a lot, don't you?"

Isabel shrugged. "I do. But I'd rather have a healthy knee. Otherwise, how could I keep up with my four awesomely best *chicas*."

Charlotte understood. Sometimes she missed traveling, but right now, she wouldn't trade the friendships she had made for anything. She just knew the BSG would be friends forever.

"OK, your cartoon is in. My feature is finished, as well as the rest of the seventh-grade page. We can both relax and enjoy the 'shopping experience.' I called my Dad and he said he'd meet us at the store, too. I hope he remembers. He's been acting like one of the original absent-minded professors lately. I've been wondering if he has a new project going on … he always acts a little spacey when he's starting a new book," Charlotte said, a hint of nervousness creeping into her voice.

Isabel looked up at her friend. Did a new book mean a new place for Charlotte? She hoped not. The Beacon Street Girls without Charlotte just wouldn't be right. They had had that scare already, when Mr. Ramsey considered moving to England for work.

"I can't buy that much today," Isabel admitted. "But Candice's boots are a perfect fit. Let's look at the list again."

Charlotte had it folded in her purse. She pulled it out, smoothed the creases, and began to read out loud:

 ABIGAIL ADAMS JUNIOR HIGH

 OFFICIAL LAKE RESCUE SUPPLY LIST

Must Have:
- ☐ Hiking boots. (Highly recommended. Too easy to turn an ankle wearing sneakers, especially if it's muddy.)
- ☐ Two pairs of jeans or cargo pants, not new
- ☐ Two t-shirts
- ☐ Two sweatshirts
- ☐ Jacket or a warm coat
- ☐ Rain slicker
- ☐ One hat or baseball cap
- ☐ One or two pairs of shorts
- ☐ Six pairs of socks and underclothes
- ☐ Two bandanas
- ☐ Tennis shoes and water shoes for night or canoe
- ☐ Pajamas and personal items for overnight
- ☐ Sunscreen
- ☐ Bug repellant
- ☐ Notebook
- ☐ New journal (a spiral notebook is fine)
- ☐ Several pens

Nice to have:
- ☐ Binoculars
- ☐ Identification books to record birds, trees, flowers, animals in area

Extras:
- ☐ Cameras, a paperback book
- ☐ Personal snack food, things like: Energy bars, pretzels, fruit roll-ups

"Hiking boots. (Highly recommended. Too easy to turn an ankle wearing sneakers, especially if it's muddy.)"

"It will rain if I go." Isabel sighed. "I'm a rain magnet."

"Since my specialty is disasters of all kinds," Charlotte laughed, "I'll have to get boots so I can cross sprained ankle off my list of things that might happen while we're there."

"Two pairs of jeans or cargo pants, not new"

"Why can't they be new?" Isabel wondered.

"Blisters. And new jeans can feel like wearing sandpaper when you're hiking or when you get wet. Trust me. This is the voice of experience speaking. Besides, they'll get wrecked."

"You know so much about travel, Charlotte," noted Isabel. "Maybe we should write a book together when we grow up, and I could do all the illustrations. We could go around the world. We'd be a great team."

"That would be my *dream* job," Charlotte exclaimed. "We should totally do that right after college. My friend Anabel in Australia has an older sister who backpacked around the world for a whole year after she graduated from the University of Sydney. We could stay in hostels and ..."

"Backpacks?" Isabel questioned. "How about a suitcase with rollers and cheap hotels?"

"Well, it depends how famous our books get." Charlotte grinned, picked up her supply list and continued to read:

" - Two pairs of jeans or cargo pants, not new
- Two t-shirts
- Two sweatshirts
- Jacket or a warm coat

- Rain slicker
- One hat or baseball cap
- One or two pairs of shorts
- Six pairs of socks and underclothes"

"Why six socks and underwear?" Isabel said. "For four days?"

"I don't know about you, but do you know how many times I can fall out of a canoe without even trying?" Charlotte asked.

Isabel hoped she was exaggerating.

" *- Two bandanas*
- Tennis shoes and water shoes for night or canoe
- Pajamas and personal items for overnight
- Sunscreen
- Bug repellant

"That's a given." Charlotte made a face. "If we're near a lake the mosquitoes can be as big as hummingbirds."

"I thought mosquitoes were gone by now."

"You never know," said Charlotte. "They can be devious little creatures. And I'm not taking any chances." She picked up a medium-sized bottle of "Bug Off."

" *- Notebook*
- New journal (a spiral notebook is fine)
- Several pens

Nice to have:
- Binoculars
- Identification books to record birds, trees, flowers,
animals in area

Extras:
- Cameras, a paperback book"

"What kind of animals? I hope we see a moose." Isabel set her backpack down. "Where is everyone? Are we in the right place to meet them? My horoscope said I was going to make a mistake today, but that it wasn't really my fault. I hope this isn't it."

"I thought we were meeting here. But I was distracted this morning. Maybe everyone said lockers. They'll find us. I think by animals, they mean mice or groundhogs or maybe snakes, bears, squirrels."

Charlotte had buried the word bear in with the rest of the animals she could think of, but Isabel jumped on it.

"Won't real bears be hibernating?" Isabel asked.

"It's probably too early. They're still eating, but they only eat berries, don't they?" Charlotte laughed and kept reading:

"Personal snack food, things like:
- Energy bars, pretzels, fruit roll-ups"

"Here you two are." Katani, Avery, and Maeve hurried up beside them. "I thought we were meeting at the office. Remember, my grandmother was giving me some money."

"We said the front steps last time I heard," Charlotte smiled.

Mrs. Summers pulled up to the curb, waved from her

mini-van, and the girls piled in, tossing their gear in the back.

"Charlotte, Charlotte, sit by me," Kelley pleaded from the very back seat. She clutched Mr. Bear in one hand and patted the seat beside her with the other. "You are my best friend in the whole world, besides Mr. Bear. Marty is my favorite, too, but he isn't a bear," she stated matter-of-factly.

"Almost," Avery said. "Marty is cute as a little bear cub. We should have told your dad to bring him, Char."

"To the mall? No way." Charlotte let pictures flash through her mind of Marty, the wonder dog, loose in the mall. They could probably catch him easily, though, since he'd stop to let everyone pet him.

Kelley put her arm around Charlotte and hugged her tight. She loved everyone, and most of the time, everyone loved her.

"Everyone have her seat belt fastened?" Mrs. Summers called, looking in the rear mirror. "We're off on an adventure."

They were a tight fit but giggling helped, and they weren't going far. "Good thing I didn't eat too much for dinner last night," Katani said.

"You did too, Katani," said Kelley. "You ate fish and broccoli, and rice and pumpkin pie."

That set them giggling again. Kelley was very literal. She said things exactly as they were.

Maeve piped in. "My mom made the best dinner—roast chicken with mashed potatoes and gravy. It's my favorite dinner in the world. I could eat it every night."

Charlotte laughed. Everything with Maeve was extreme. Things were the best, the most fabulous, or the absolute worst. It really made hanging out with her fun—it was kind of like having a character in a sitcom for a friend.

Mr. Ramsey was waiting for them in front of the outdoor

store. Charlotte waved to him. When he had heard Mrs. Summers was taking all of the girls shopping for the trip, he called to ask if he could come along. Mr. Ramsey loved to plan trips ... even for other people. He rubbed his hands together and said, "OK, girls, big-time shopping. Let's get started. Thanks for picking them up, Mrs. Summers."

"Nadine, please, and I wouldn't miss this trip for anything. I helped outfit my two oldest girls for the last big Lake Rescue weekend. If we get separated, we'll meet back at shoes. That's easy to find."

The BSG hurried off together. "I have to wear all my sisters' hand-me-downs," Katani complained. "Is that a major drag or what?"

"All of them?" Maeve said. "You can't have anything new?"

"I can, but I have to buy a lot myself. I thought maybe I could afford a new vest and some socks." Katani flipped through a circular display of vests, most of them plain blue, plain brown, plain tan.

"Look!" Charlotte pulled a khaki vest from the revolving rack. "This is almost as good as a photographer's vest with all the pockets. I hate having anything in my hands when I hike. My old shorts have good pockets and with a small backpack, I should be—"

"Free to catch yourself if you fall." Avery finished the sentence.

Charlotte looked at Avery with a hurt expression. "Well, that too. You know, Avery, I'm not a klutz at *everything* I do. My dad and I have hiked around a lot of places."

"I know that, Char ... you know me. Open mouth, make joke, insert foot," apologized Avery.

"Cool!" Katani had wandered off to a rack that held

more colorful clothing. "Look! This looks just like a Juicy Couture vest."

"If Juicy designs vests." Isabel smiled. "It is cute. Is it lots more expensive than the plain ones?"

"I'm afraid to look." Katani pulled out the price tag and her face fell at least a couple of inches. "Yeah, it is."

"Your mother is talking to my dad and smiling," Charlotte pointed out. "My dad almost always puts people in a good mood."

Katani didn't hesitate long. "Won't hurt to try." She took off with the vest to plead her case.

They moved toward shoes. Katani caught up. "Mom said OK, she'd advance me money, but I have to pay it back. At this rate, I'm going to be baby-sitting for about a year without pay. But it's worth it. If I'm going to help Isabel make pajamas for us all, I don't have time to sew a vest. Do you think I can find orange socks to match?"

"Go for it. But bright colors attract rattlesnakes," said Avery with a mischievous grin.

Katani stopped and stared at Avery. "That's not true. I know that's not true." She acted, though, as if she wasn't positive that Avery was teasing her.

"Well," interrupted Charlotte, "I don't know about snakes, but I do know that bright colors attract bees."

"That's true, but I went on hikesafe.com. It said you should wear bright clothes so people can see you in the woods," said Avery. "So actually, Katani, your vest is a good idea."

"I have no hiking boots," Maeve said. "Help me look, Charlotte. You're buying boots, aren't you? I'm not sure what to get."

Charlotte nodded. She hadn't packed her old boots when they left Paris. She looked around. Where to start? The store must have a million styles. Methodically, she made her way up one aisle and down another. Nope. No way. Maybe. Too expensive. Not at all practical. Her father followed her, but he waited for her to pick out some to try on.

"I keep thinking of what we'd need if we were in Africa or Australia," he said. "You will need shoes suited for climbing in the mountains. Then again, we haven't planned next summer's vacation. We could go someplace wonderful to hike. Like the Grand Canyon, or the Appalachian Trail."

"That would be so fun, Dad. Start collecting information." A trip with her father was always an adventure. "Will you teach summer school?"

"Not if I can work on my new book. How about these?" Her father pulled a pair of medium high-tops off the shelf. They were a nice combination of dark brown and tan. "Try them on."

Charlotte sat on a chair and piled her collection of clothes next to her. Before she could get her shoes off, Maeve showed up waving hot pink boots. "Look, Char, look! Aren't these the best? Ms. Razzberry Pink will freak out when she sees them." Maeve was a big fan of "Think Pink," Razzberry's store for everything pink.

"Sit here by Charlotte and try them on, Maeve," said Mr. Ramsey.

Once Maeve was wearing them, she jumped up and walked up and down the aisle. She looked in one floor mirror, then another.

"Does the sole feel very thick, Maeve? They don't look as if they have lug soles at all, but flat ones. They might be a little slick walking in mud or rain. And I think your feet will get cold and wet quickly with so much canvas instead of leather on the sides."

Mr. Ramsey made his argument against the pink boots without saying no way will those work. Maeve walked around a bit more. "I guess they are more for fun than for hiking. But they're *so* Elle Woods." Elle was one of Maeve's favorite movie characters from one of her all-time favorite movies, *Legally Blonde*.

"Look at what I'm getting, Maeve." Charlotte held up one foot. "What if you got something like this in charcoal gray and then replaced the shoelaces with some pink ones?"

Maeve tried on a pair of boots like Charlotte's and walked around. "I see what your dad means. These feel much sturdier. But I hate being so practical. It's just not my style."

Mr. Ramsey disappeared, then showed up again holding a pair of hot pink shoelaces. "Look here, on the package." He pointed to some writing that actually said, "Guaranteed not to be practical or even dorky."

"Those are fabulous!" Maeve took the laces and placed them against the boots. "Thanks, Mr. Ramsey."

Mr. Ramsey, Maeve, and Charlotte walked over to where Isabel and Katani were mesmerized by a book with lots of colored pictures ... of snakes. Maeve looked over their shoulders. "Where are the New Hampshire snakes?"

Avery walked up behind them. "Most snakes are as afraid of you as you are of them. They get out of the way fast if they have time." Avery spoke authoritatively. She knew a lot about snakes because she kept one, Walter, as a pet.

"That's very true, Avery," Mr. Ramsey concurred.

"I think you wear a bell," Kelley said, hugging Mr. Bear tighter.

"No, that's for bears." Dillon Johnson interjected out of nowhere. "Did you get your bear bell, Maeve?"

"No, I plan to send you ahead on the trail."

"Are you here alone?" Charlotte asked Dillon.

"I think Nick and Sammy went home already. I was on my way out when I heard a familiar shriek."

"OK, OK, don't let us keep you from your mission." Maeve turned around and headed for the warm clothing section as if seeing Dillon at the outdoor store was no big deal at all.

But Charlotte could guess how fast Maeve's heart was beating as she walked away. Dillon caught up and acted as if he was going to stay with them until they finished shopping.

"Look," he whispered to Maeve and the rest of the BSG who had caught up. "I think that's a bear right up there in the coat department."

"Dillon, that's so mean," Maeve scolded Dillon.

The "bear" Dillon had pointed out was Chelsea Briggs, trying to fit into a brown fleece coat in the juniors' department of the sporting goods store.

Charlotte caught Chelsea's eye. It was an uncomfortable moment. Charlotte felt terrible for her classmate's predicament. Because the word "embarrassed" was her middle name, Charlotte wouldn't wish public humiliation on her worst enemy. She began to quickly walk away hoping everyone would follow her. Isabel caught on, pulling Maeve in a different direction. Dillon followed, but not without looking back.

"No, I was wrong, that's Chelsea Bigg."

"That's really mean, Dillon," Maeve said, in a firm voice. "Let's go, girls. We have shopping to do." Dillon's smile faded and he looked as if he'd been given the big brush-off, which, of course, he had. Fortunately, he took the hint.

Charlotte looked around and, to her dismay, found that her friends had turned into the children's coats section.

"These are little kids' coats," Kelley said, not understanding why they had made the detour. "We are not little children, Charlotte Ramsey," she said firmly. "We want to go over there." She pointed toward where Chelsea and her mother were talking.

"It's OK, Kelley," Charlotte said, putting her arm around Kelley. "I went the wrong way. We'll go the right way in just a minute. Do you think Mr. Bear needs a new coat?"

"No, his coat is warm." Kelley laughed at her own joke.

"Mother, come on. I told you this wouldn't work." Chelsea's voice, full of frustration, floated over the racks toward where the BSG were trying to hide. "Nothing here is ever going to fit me. This is extra large. I'll wear my old coat."

"But it's too small, too, Chelsea, and not nearly warm enough for a night outside near a lake. What if it rains? We could even have an early snow. I wanted to get you a new coat this fall anyway."

"OK, what do *you* suggest we do?"

Charlotte could hear the frustration in Chelsea's voice. She sounded close to tears.

"We'll go over to the boys' section. They'll have all the same styles, maybe just not the colors. Put that one back. Come on, it's no big deal. You have to have a coat."

There was no way the BSG could hide, no way for Chelsea not to see them, since the way to the boys' and men's coats was past the aisle of children's coats right in front of where they were standing. All they could do was pretend they didn't see her.

"Chelsea, hi, Chelsea." Kelley knew Chelsea. Everyone at Abigail Adams school knew Kelley. A few really immature boys teased Kelley on occasion. But most of the kids looked out for her, helped her if she got lost, or lost Mr. Bear, which happened a lot, way too often. Unfortunately, Kelley didn't realize that, at that moment, Chelsea wanted to be invisible.

Chelsea looked to see the BSG huddled in a tight group, looking rather foolish. "Hi, Kelley," Chelsea said, then hurried to catch up with her mother.

"OMG," Maeve said. "How embarrassing."

"For who?" Charlotte pointed out. "Us or Chelsea Briggs?"

"What could we do?" Avery said. "Come on. I have to have a new coat."

Those who were getting new fleece jackets went about their selections with less enthusiasm than they had for vests and boots and pink shoelaces. The jacket selection had been picked over and the colors were kind of drab. But Avery didn't care, and Charlotte found a nice, cozy gray one. They finished their shopping quickly.

"We'll stop at Village Fare and get pizza for the sleep-over tonight. OK with you, girls?" Mr. Ramsey asked.

"I guess no one wants anchovies?" Avery asked hopefully.

"No, Avery," four girls said together.

"No one wants anchovies. But for you ... half with anchovies," added Charlotte.

The girls planned to meet at Charlotte's in an hour. Katani, Isabel, Avery, and Maeve waved to Charlotte and Mr. Ramsey and jumped into Mrs. Summers' car. As they drove off, a light rain began to fall.

Completely mortified. Utterly embarrassed. Totally humiliated. What's my favorite? Maybe all three — completelymortifiedutterlyembarrassedtotallyhumiliated.

I thought I would be safe going shopping right after school with Mom ... no way was I going out with the crowds on Saturday — too big a chance of running into people from A. A. Jr. High.

HA! Obviously, the plan didn't work. I didn't even have to hear what that dork, Dillon, was saying about me ... and then it got worse. The Beacon Street Girls were trying to HIDE from me because they knew I was embarrassed. When people are embarrassed that you are embarrassed, it just makes the whole thing ten times more embarrassing. I hate when people feel sorry for me.

But that was only half the problem. The major thing was that none of the juniors' coats would fit me, so I am going to be wearing a boy's coat at Lake Rescue. Lucky me. Even if no one else can tell where it came from, I'LL know. I hate the whole fashion thing. What's with not making cute outdoor clothes for bigger girls? I wouldn't mind wearing bright purple instead of gray. Don't we all deserve to look good? I've seen all those plus-size models look amazing, but they have their clothes tailored for them. What about the regular people?

Anyway, things are not looking good for Lake Rescue. I mean, the BSG (that's what everyone calls them now) are actually nice, and I felt bad around them. What's going to happen when I have to be around some of the meanest people in the class?

I can't believe I have to go camping with Kiki Underwood and the Queens of Mean. I can feel disaster brewing. Maybe I should tell Mom that I want to go to Grandma's instead. She'll like that.

Signed,

Chelsea Briggs ☆
    ☆ photographer to the Stars, etc.

CHAPTER **6**

CR

THE SLEEPOVER

CHARLOTTE and her dad stopped at Village Fare on the way home and bought three different kinds of pizza. The fragrant smell of tomato sauce, yeasty bread dough, and pepperoni filled the car.

"Is that pizza I smell?" Miss Pierce, their landlady, stuck her head out of her door as they came in.

"Sure is." Charlotte's dad laughed. "We have plenty. Care to join us, Miss Pierce?"

"My nose says yes, but my stomach knows better." Miss Pierce laughed. "Pizza is for young stomachs."

"Or those of cast iron, like my dad's." Charlotte juggled two of the pizzas and her bag of school books, thinking she should have made two trips.

The Ramseys hadn't done a major house cleaning since the last time the BSG came over for a sleepover, so Charlotte looked around to make sure things weren't in too big a mess.

Charlotte and Marty waited for Katani, Maeve, Isabel, and Avery on the porch swing. This was partly an excuse to be outside for a few minutes, and partly an opportunity to

❀

try out the new fleece coat. It was so warm and snuggly. Charlotte didn't mind that it was gray. Katani could have the bright colors. She loved running her hands over the soft material, knowing it was going to be perfect for the outdoor camping adventure.

No moon and no sounds in the neighborhood, combined with a misty rain, created an atmosphere that made Charlotte shiver. Maybe this was what Lake Rescue would feel like at night—misty and mysterious. Marty jumped up beside her on the swing and looked at her as if to say, Is anything wrong?

"The only thing wrong is that if you put your muddy paws on my coat, you're in serious trouble." Leave it to Marty to destroy a spooky atmosphere.

Suddenly, four girls tumbled into the yard, pushing and shoving, laughing and squealing. They had walked over together. Mrs. Kaplan used to drive Maeve everywhere, to make sure she got places safely, but she didn't have time now that she had started to work.

"What are you doing sitting out here in the rain?" Avery asked.

"Oh, just trying out my new coat." Charlotte stood up and led the way into the big house.

"It'll be perfect for sitting beside a roaring fire, telling ghost stories, while you're all toasty warm by yourself. I think it sounds very romantic." Katani carried her suitcase up the broad staircase.

"I wouldn't say you were exactly an expert on romance, Katani, lugging that big suitcase up these stairs instead of floating down them in a satin ball gown," Maeve teased. She couldn't resist setting down her things and floating back to the bottom, just for practice in case she was ever in a movie that called for floating.

Avery zipped down the banister, squealing, then collapsed with laughter as she reached the bottom. "You know, Charlotte, you should get up fifteen minutes earlier every day and run up and down these stairs before school. You'd be in really good shape for the trip."

"I'd rather just hike up a mountain ... more interesting." Charlotte hoped she would be in good enough shape to hike up the mountain at Lake Rescue. She hadn't been hiking in so long.

The pizzas disappeared in a very short time. Marty sat back on his haunches and waved his front feet, begging for handouts.

"Charlotte, let's go," Avery said impatiently.

"OK, Tower trek is on!" Charlotte had her own overnight bag packed so she wouldn't have to keep running back and forth to her room.

"We're ready." Katani and Isabel led the way, followed by a barking, dancing Marty.

"What's the program for tonight?" questioned Avery.

"I have a lot of items on my list, but mainly we have to choose what pajamas to wear for Pajama Day."

Isabel agreed. "We've waited way too long. If Katani and I are going to make them, we have to pick something simple."

The BSG had made the Tower into their special hangout. Since the Tower had only four window seats, and there were five BSG, Isabel had recently created her own space. She hung a hoop from the ceiling and attached it to pieces of fabric that opened up into a flower. She had painted a beautiful compass rose on the floor with the names of all the BSG. Now the Tower was really complete, and the girls felt like it was their second home.

Charlotte had all her things in their usual places. After all, it was her house, and where she came most afternoons to write.

They arranged their sleeping bags and got into their pajamas. As soon as they settled down, Marty curled round and round and round, finally found a good spot, and nodded off. Avery, President of the BSG, cleared her throat and called the meeting to order: "I hereby call this official BSG meeting to order. Keeper of the Records ... what is on tonight's agenda?"

Maeve giggled at Avery's serious voice and threw a pillow at her head. Charlotte ripped a piece of paper from her notebook and read aloud:

```
Tonight's list of things we need to do:
-  Decide what kind of pajamas to wear on
   Pajama Day.
-  Decide what clothes to take on the
   camping trip.
-  Decide how to make the pjs.
```

"I still can't believe that I am going on a camping trip," Maeve said. "You'd think my mother would be soooo happy to have me stay home and study."

"And you would be soooo bored, and wondering what we all were doing the entire time." Avery laughed. "Think how much you'd miss us."

"Yeah, that's true." Maeve started twisting her hair into a hair clip. "Besides," she said dramatically, "what would you even do without the redhead? I'll stand out in the woods."

"Will you ever," said Avery, looking at Maeve in her bright pink nightgown and big fuzzy slippers.

"Personally," Katani added, "I'm really looking forward

to spending quality time with the Queens of Mean in scenic New Hampshire. Do you think they like fishing, camping, climbing mountains, or hanging out on the hard, cold, rocky ground? I can just hear Anna and Joline's whines now."

"Maybe we can play tricks on the boys ... I've thought of a dozen so far," said Avery.

Charlotte listened for a little while, a warm glow of anticipation growing inside. She was ready to leave tomorrow, or at least Monday. She wasn't sure what to expect on her first big junior high trip, but that was part of the fun. After all, anything was possible on an adventure, she reminded herself.

"We'd better do first things first. Pajamas. Any ideas?" asked Katani.

"Definitely not silky stuff like what Maeve and Katani are wearing right now," Avery said. "Too cheesy."

"Oh, Avery, I suppose you'd like a one-piece flannel pj number with feet." Katani stood up and modeled the new peach-colored nightgown she'd designed and sewn the week before.

"What's wrong with flannel? We're wearing them to school, remember?" Avery was wearing flannel with stripes. Flannel was so practical and snuggly.

"Over our clothes," Isabel added. "We'll have to make them a little bigger than our sizes."

"Stripes!" Maeve squealed. "I have an idea. Let's make flannel pjs with black stripes like one of those old prisoner uniforms."

Since Maeve had lived all her life over the Movie House, she had seen practically every movie ever made. Sometimes her movie information came in handy, or made for interesting bedtime stories.

Everyone stared at Maeve for a couple of beats, then

started to laugh. "That would be unique," Avery said. "We might even win one of the prizes."

"Hey, let's wear signs on our backs. Like, THIS SCHOOL IS A PRISON," added Avery. She printed the sign ideas on their chalkboard.

"HELP US ESCAPE THE BIG HOUSE." Maeve giggled. "They called prison 'the big house' in really old movies."

"ONLY FIVE YEARS LEFT IN MY SENTENCE." Isabel counted on her fingers. "Eighth, ninth, tenth, eleventh, twelfth. That's five."

"And more than half of this year left." Avery took a drink from the bottled water she pulled from her bag.

"What if we chained ourselves together like a chain gang?" Maeve was thinking. "*The Defiant Ones* with Sidney Poitier and Tony Curtis had them chained together. They escaped that way, and they hated each other, but because they had to work together to escape they became friends."

"Maeve, do you really think we could get through a whole day all chained together?" Avery fell over laughing and pretty soon everyone was thinking of bad-case scenarios.

"Charlotte would trip in the cafeteria and we'd all fall, dumping food on hundreds of unsuspecting diners," Katani teased gently.

"No one would be unsuspecting if I was in the chain gang. They'd be watching us the entire time we were trying to walk to a table." Charlotte could laugh at herself by now. After all, her now-famous disaster ultimately led to her having three new friends, now grown to four.

"If Maeve fell off the climbing ropes again, she'd pull us all down with her."

"Yeah, Dillon wouldn't be able to save us all."

"What about this? How many girls can you fit in front of

a mirror to reapply lip gloss?" asked Katani, hands on hips.

The last idea topped all the funny pictures and put an end to any possibility of a chain gang.

"But, hey, what about this?" Avery said. "I'll bet I can find black balloons at Party Favors. You know, like we're each fastened to a ball and chain."

"A paper chain would break." Katani thought for a second. "I know. We can make chains from black electric tape and tape the balloons to our socks."

"Great idea," Isabel said, laughing.

"OK, is everyone in favor of prison pajamas?" Charlotte asked.

"Sure," everyone agreed. "It's a really funny idea," Katani said.

"And let's take the pajamas with us to camp. They'll be warm if we get flannel," Avery added.

"Next agenda?" Charlotte moved onto her sleeping bag, tired of standing by the chalkboard.

Maeve started brushing Isabel's long, black hair. "Can you believe that Chelsea Briggs couldn't fit into any of the coats in the juniors' section of the sporting goods store?"

"I felt kind of sorry for her, having us see her go to the boys' department," Charlotte added. "It must be hard to be that heavy."

"Why doesn't she lose some weight?" Avery suggested. "Maybe if she got more exercise, she could get in shape."

"Or tried eating less," Maeve said.

"I wonder if she can handle the ropes course at the camp," Avery said. "If she's out of shape, she probably won't be able to lift her own weight."

"We shouldn't be talking about someone's weight," Katani said. "It's kind of mean and it's really none of our business.

We don't even know why she is overweight anyway."

"It might be important if she was your partner or something. You know how they keep saying this camp is to teach us to work together." Avery thought about it. "What if she started slipping off the ropes and I was her partner? Besides, people talk about my being short all the time. What's the difference if we talk about her? No one is hearing us."

"Being short and being fat are two really different things, Avery." Maeve got out some new body lotion and shook it. "I was kind of chubby in the fourth grade. People called me mudgy, pudgy, Maeve." Maeve blew out her cheeks, stood up and wobbled around as if she was too heavy to stand up.

She was such a good actress, no one could keep from laughing.

"What happened?" Isabel asked.

"I grew four inches overnight. I guess it was baby fat. It went away. But I'll tell you, I didn't like the name-calling one bit. It totally hurt my feelings, and I can still remember crying about it to my mom."

"Well," said Isabel sympathetically, "Just think about Chelsea. Her weight's still there. She probably feels really bad sometimes."

The idea of Maeve ever being chubby was hard to imagine, but Charlotte didn't feel comfortable talking about Chelsea Briggs any more. Chelsea was nice to work with and she was glad when Avery changed the subject.

"Who's going to walk Marty while we're gone?" Avery had let the little dog curl in her lap. Now she picked him up and rubbed noses with him. He was too sleepy to protest or even show off. "Did everyone give Marty a piece of pizza?" she asked. "Dogs shouldn't have that much people food."

"Hey, pizza is a major food group," Charlotte said. "I

wish we'd left some for a midnight snack."

Maeve had a suggestion. "How about we ask Razzberry Pink to take Marty for a walk with La Fanny ... Marty loves that poodle. He thinks she is his girlfriend." She waved her left hand covered with new raspberry swirl nail polish. The sweet pungent scent surrounded them.

"I have to open the window, Maeve. That stuff smells like poison," Avery coughed.

"Never mind, I'm done." Maeve put her polish away.

"Maybe Dad can take him to classes at the university," Charlotte decided. "He's done that before when he doesn't have to work in the library. The students love Marty almost as much as we do. They play Frisbee with him."

A long week, filled with schoolwork and news about the camping trip and Pajama Day, not to mention the cozy warm Tower room and stomachs full of pizza, began to get to the usually energetic girls.

They talked a little about what they were going to pack for camp, but soon their voices trailed off.

Charlotte had put on one of their favorite CDs—the Beatles Greatest Hits, which belonged to her father. Within a few minutes, Paul McCartney's "Hey, Jude" was singing them to sleep.

Soft sobbing from Isabel brought them awake again.

"Isabel, is that you crying?" Katani asked. "What's the matter?"

"Oh, I think I've made a terrible mistake." Isabel sat up and rubbed her eyes with a tissue.

"Is your mother worse?" asked Maeve.

"Oh, no, in fact, she's much better. Moving here, working with the new doctors has helped her so much. I—I—"

"You can tell us, Isabel." Charlotte moved around and put

her arm around Isabel's shoulder. "We'll try to help if we can."

"It's my cartoon."

"Your cartoon? The one you drew for this week's newspaper?" Charlotte asked. "You said you turned it in."

"I did. That's the problem. I didn't mean anything by it. It was before—before—"

"Before what?" Avery was fully awake now and a little impatient.

"My cartoon was about the camping trip. And I—well, I drew a fat bear sneaking up on people sitting at the campfire. It was before. I drew it before we saw Chelsea today. But she won't know that. What if she, what if she thinks she's the fat bear? That I was making fun of her?"

"Maybe she won't even notice," Maeve said. "How could she think the bear was her anyway?"

"Don't you remember?" Avery asked. "Dillon said, 'Look, it's a bear.' You know, when she was trying to get into that fleece coat. I'm sure she heard him say that."

"Oh, yeah. Dillon." Maeve frowned. She wasn't happy with the way he spoke about Chelsea. She thought it was so mean to make fun of someone like that.

"I know what, Isabel." Katani had an idea. "I really don't know when the newspaper is printed. But maybe not till morning. I'll talk to my grandmother first thing when I get home. I have to go home really early to stay with Kelley. I'll tell her to pull the cartoon. Run something else about the trip. A map or something."

"Do you think she could?" Isabel stopped crying and sniffed hopefully.

"I'll tell her it's really important, an emergency. I know she'll try. Stop worrying, and let's all of us go to sleep or I'll never get up at all."

Charlotte lay awake thinking for a little while. The camping trip was supposed to help them all to get along and learn to work together. The Beacon Street Girls had done that on their own. After those first days of school when they had practically hated each other, they had become the type of close-knit friends that would do anything for each other. They were like the five Musketeers, Charlotte felt. One girl's problem was every girl's problem.

✿

All of a sudden, Charlotte's eyes popped open. She realized that she hadn't written to Sophie, her best friend in Paris, for some time. Things had been so busy. She didn't want Sophie to think she had been forgotten. She hoped that Sophie understood that Charlotte missed her. Sometimes it was hard to keep in touch, but she and Sophie were true friends ... they were always able to pick up right where they had left off.

CHAPTER 7

ભ

MAJOR FAUX PAS

CHELSEA BRIGGS hurried down the hall, her tote bag full of photos to show Mrs. Fields. She hoped she hadn't picked out too many. She realized the principal didn't have all day to sit looking at the Chelsea Briggs personal photography collection. Even though she said she wanted to see some samples, Mrs. Fields might have just been being nice.

Passing *The Sentinel* office, she grabbed a newspaper from the stack outside the door, tucked it under her arm, juggled her books and the bag of photos, and ducked into the office.

"Hi, Chelsea," Ms. Sahni said. "Looking forward to the camping trip?"

Why did everybody think that going to the woods of New Hampshire to make giant fools of themselves playing *Survivor* was the biggest event of the year?

"Not really. I'm not much of a camper. Mrs. Fields here?"

"Yes, I'll ask if she can see you." Ms. Sahni smiled and nodded toward a chair. Chelsea was afraid if she sat down and got up again quickly, she'd spill everything. So she just

✿

stood there … feeling like a coat stand.

In less than a minute, Ruby Fields came out of her office. She smiled as if she'd been waiting to see Chelsea all day. "You look like you could use some help here." She offered to take one of Chelsea's bags.

"I brought some samples of my photos like you asked me to do. It's too many, but you can just glance at them."

"Oh, I'm eager to see them. I'm glad you remembered." Mrs. Fields led Chelsea back into her office and closed the door. She motioned to a chair, and while Chelsea got settled, she opened the manila envelope.

When Chelsea saw Mrs. Fields was actually going to take each one out and look at it carefully, she relaxed, but still felt nervous. So, she pulled *The Sentinel* from under her arm and opened it to the seventh-grade page. She looked forward to Charlotte Ramsey's feature article, but should she save it for last or read it first? She did neither.

A wave of heat started at her toes and flashed straight up her body. Fire singed her heart, sent it thumping, and kept going, making her feel faint.

"Oh!" She managed a sound between a squeal and a gasp. Tears rolled down her cheeks faster than she could brush them away.

"Why, Chelsea, what's the matter? Are you all right?"

All Chelsea could do was shake her head and turn a bright shade of red.

Mrs. Fields handed her a tissue and waited.

Finally, Chelsea handed Mrs. Fields the wadded, damp page of the paper and pointed to the cartoon.

Mrs. Fields studied it for a couple of seconds. "Isabel Martinez is such a good artist. And I think she captured the major thing everyone is worried about at camp. Bears. Don't worry, Chelsea, there hasn't been a bear sighting at Lake Rescue in a very long time. The rangers work very hard at keeping the bears away from camp."

"No, that's not a bear, that's me!" Chelsea's sudden anger helped her stop crying. "How could she do that to me? Why?"

Mrs. Fields laid the cartoon between them. Isabel had drawn a cute, chubby bear sneaking up on the campfire, where a bunch of kids sat listening to a ghost story. She had made it seem that the bear wanted to hear the story, too.

Ruby Fields studied Chelsea. "Chelsea, why would you think this bear is supposed to be you?"

"Friday. Friday at the sporting goods store ..." Chelsea filled Mrs. Fields in on the incident.

"I guess I can see how you might assume that, Chelsea. But let's not jump to conclusions here. I can't imagine that Isabel Martinez would ever deliberately do anything to hurt you. But if it will make you feel any better, I'll talk to her. It's too late to do anything right now. All the copies have been handed out."

That was what Chelsea was afraid of. And by now, they all would have heard the "coat" story and Dillon's remark. Suddenly, Chelsea hated Dillon Johnson. Why did he have to make a joke like that?

Mrs. Fields could see that Chelsea was growing more upset. She handed her another tissue and said, "Chelsea, let's change the subject for a minute. You have a real talent for capturing the essence of a person on film. I'm going to ask Ms. Weston to let you be the official photographer for the camping trip. I can't think of anyone who'd do a better job. We'll certainly pay for developing the pictures."

Chelsea struggled to pull herself together. She didn't

want Mrs. Fields to think she was a complete loser. But this was hard. All those kids thinking she was the fat bear in the cartoon. She'd have to put on her Teflon coat, the one that made her immune to insults.

With her best "I can roll with the punches" smile, she said, "I'd really like that, Mrs. Fields." Just saying it made Chelsea feel more in control. Whatever happened she knew she could take some great pictures at Lake Rescue. It made her heart grow just a little lighter.

And taking photos will give me an excuse not to always do the activities, she added to herself. No one would ever believe that a person her size could hide behind a camera, but most of the time she could, and did.

"OK, we'll talk more before you leave." Mrs. Fields gathered up Chelsea's photos and placed them carefully back in the manila envelope and then into her tote bag.

○○

As soon as Chelsea was gone, Mrs. Fields sent a runner to get Isabel Martinez out of class, then asked her assistant to get her Mrs. Briggs' phone number. When she next looked up from her work, not only Isabel, but her granddaughter, Katani, stood before her, looking sheepish.

"I can tell by looking at you that you understand why I wanted to talk to you, Isabel. Why are you here, Katani?"

"I was supposed to talk to you first thing Saturday morning, but I forgot."

"OK, let's hear the story. It seems you already know I'm not pleased. Ridiculing another student will not be tolerated at Abigail Adams. You both know that."

"I didn't mean any harm, Mrs. Fields, honest I didn't," Isabel said. She started to cry. "I drew the cartoon and turned it in at the end of the day on Friday. Before we even went to the store. Before Dillon Johnson saw Chelsea Briggs trying on that brown fleece coat and called her a bear. He was making a joke, but it really wasn't funny. None of us laughed."

"At our sleepover," Katani picked up the story, "Isabel realized that her cartoon might hurt Chelsea's feelings. I told her I'd talk to you you first thing Saturday morning and see if the newspaper had gone to print. It's my fault. I forgot. I'm just so sorry. Isabel would never make fun of anyone."

Ruby Fields sighed. "I know that, Isabel. I just had to make sure. The whole thing was an unfortunate coincidence. But still, someone's feelings were hurt. Maybe only a few people will know what happened at the store. It's actually a very cute and imaginative cartoon. I love the idea of the bear not being scary at all, just wanting to hear the end of the story." Mrs. Fields looked at the cartoon again. "Someone sends *The Sentinel* to the printer right after school on Friday. Even if you had reached me on Saturday, I don't think I could have pulled the drawing."

"What can I do, Mrs. Fields?" Isabel asked. "I could give up cartooning, but I love it so much."

A hint of a smile betrayed Mrs. Fields' amusement at Isabel's dramatic declaration.

"Oh, Isabel, that should never be an option. You have a talent and you must nurture that. It's part of who you are. But cartoonists, just like writers, have a responsibility not to offend anyone. To be sensitive to feelings. The best cartoonists make fun of themselves. Do you ever read *Cathy*?"

"Not really."

"Study how she makes fun of herself, her weight, her diets, her bad habits, which are similar to everyone's bad habits. Recently she has made fun of how hard it is to get married without leaving anyone out of the planning, then move in with someone, even your new husband, and mix all your things together, as well as your dogs. She makes us laugh at ourselves. Heaven help us if we ever stop laughing at ourselves."

"Well, I'd like Chelsea to know I wasn't making fun of her. All anyone can talk about is how many bears we're going to run into at Lake Rescue. I was making fun of that. How could we be afraid of a baby bear who just wants to hear the campfire story? I should have just stuck to my birds." Isabel sighed heavily.

"The best way to clear up any misunderstanding, Isabel, is by being honest. Find Chelsea and tell her the entire story."

"I don't really know Chelsea," Isabel said, looking down at her hands.

"Me neither," Katani looked at her grandmother, hoping that Mrs. Fields wouldn't make them go find Chelsea and apologize to her. That would be so embarrassing.

Mrs Fields knew that getting seventh graders to step out of their comfort zone was always a challenge.

"Well, I think you both might find a way just to let Chelsea know that you feel bad about what happened. I know you girls will find a way that isn't 'weird.' Sometimes people who are sensitive take offense when none is meant … even when something is meant as a harmless joke."

"I tease Avery about being short every chance I get." Katani smoothed out the cartoon and folded the newspaper. "And she teases me about not being able to play basketball. And we all tease Charlotte about being a klutz all the time."

"But you knew Charlotte before you could tease her, didn't you? And she knew that you were her friend."

Katani nodded. "Yeah. Believe me, it wasn't funny at

first. I remember how mad I was when she ruined my new blouse, my best creation." Katani rolled a pencil back and forth across her grandmother's desk. "Grandma Ruby, we don't have to become best friends with Chelsea, do we? You're not asking us to do that?"

"Of course not. Being best friends just happens. She might not even want to be friends with you. But I'll bet Chelsea wouldn't mind a little friendly conversation when you all are at Lake Rescue. Do you think you girls can manage that?"

"We can, Mrs. Fields." Isabel smiled, relieved that she didn't all of a sudden have to become best friends with someone she hardly knew.

"I also promise that I will show my cartoon ahead of the printing from now on, too. Oh, but I did that. Jennifer loved it."

"OK."

Suddenly, Mrs. Fields frowned and took a better look at the way the girls were dressed. "You're trying to stay out of PE as long as possible, aren't you? I think you can just make it back if you hurry," she said to her granddaughter and Isabel.

After they shut the door, Mrs. Fields sighed and picked up the phone.

"Mrs. Briggs? It's Ruby Fields at the junior high. Chelsea's fine. I just wanted to let you know about a little incident that has left Chelsea feeling a bit vulnerable."

✿

PAJAMA PLANS

"Whew." Katani grinned. "That wasn't as bad as it could have been, and I think we just missed gym. Can you come over to my house after school? Mom said she'd take us to Fabric World. We can get a pajama pattern and the striped flannel for our pjs. If you stay for supper, maybe we can get them cut out. Then we'll split the sewing job."

"I know one thing," Isabel said. "Charlotte, Avery, and Maeve owe us some serious time in return. Should we try to teach them to sew?"

"Teach Avery to sew?" Katani laughed. I'd rather make her six pairs of pajamas."

CHAPTER 8

☙

FRENEMIES AND JAILBIRDS

Chelsea Briggs'
PERSONAL, SUPER-PRIVATE JOURNAL
NO TRESPASSING . . . Ever!

Isabel Martinez found me right after gym class. Why is gym a required class anyway? Or at least I think you should be able to decide what you want to do in gym. I would jump on a trampoline.

Isabel was all "choked up" when she came to talk to me. "Chelsea," she said. "I'm really sorry about the cartoon. I did the cartoon earlier in the day and had already turned it in just before school was out. It didn't have anything to do with what happened at the store ... honest."

I could tell that Isabel was telling the truth, but I really hate when people feel sorry for me. I found myself trying to make her feel better about the whole mess. I told her after I looked at the cartoon again, I thought it was brilliant. I used that very word, brilliant. I don't know

❁

why I said brilliant. I mean the cartoon was cute and all but both Isabel and I knew it wasn't brilliant. She looked at me kind of weird when I said it.

Then she just stood there looking at me. What the heck was I supposed to do ... make her feel better? Then I did something I never do. I reached out and hugged her. She hugged back. "It's OK Isabel. I think I can bear the joke."

Isabel actually laughed. "You're funny, Chelsea."

I smiled at her, she smiled at me, blah, blah, then both of us started laughing 'cause we both knew that the whole thing was getting ridiculous. Then she turned, gave me a thumbs up, and headed back to class. She had paint on the back of her shirt. I like that in a person.

If Isabel likes art, maybe she'd like photography. Photographers and cartoonists are both artists.

I have tried to get out of going to camp, but everyone says it will be good for me. Why do all adults think they know exactly what is good for a twelve year-old? Camp will be like having PE all day, every day, for days on end with bears. I wonder if I can get sick between now and the day we leave? No, the photos. Don't forget the photos, Chelsea. Oh yeah. A job. I'll just think of it as another job.

If I'm assigned a cabin with Isabel and Charlotte, that might be all right. But with my luck, I'll have to bunk with the Queens of Mean, Anna and Joline ... or worse, Kiki Underwood. They'll think of some nickname—I've heard them all—to call me. Like Tweedle Dee or Tweedle Dum. Hey, what if we have to do something like three-legged races and I'm paired with Joline, and I trip and fall on her? I'll say, "Oh, excuse me, Ms. Perfect, with the size 1 heart, did I hurt you? Well, excuuuse me."

"Chelsea, are you still awake?" Chelsea's mother was standing at her door. "Honey, you need to get your beauty sleep. I'm sorry I'm late tonight, but I had a really important client on the line."

"Did you close your deal?" Chelsea put her journal in her desk drawer, locked it, and put the key back on the chain around her neck. Her mom worked really hard.

"I sure did. We can afford a great vacation this summer. Start thinking about where you want to go. Hey, let's you and me go to one of those beauty spas where they help you lose some weight, pamper you with massages and salt rubs and seaweed packs—"

"I'd rather go to Disney World."

"But we could be miserable together and come home two sizes, maybe three sizes smaller. We'd have to buy all new clothes and—"

"Good night, Mom." Chelsea hugged her mother, got in bed, and turned over, as if to go to sleep.

Her mother took the hint, left Chelsea's room, and turned off the light as she left.

That left Chelsea to lie in bed and think, a very bad late night habit she had developed lately. She knew her mother loved her to pieces and would do anything for her. But she just wished her mom would lay off the weight thing. Her mom was obsessed that Chelsea would get diabetes like her grandfather. And maybe she was embarrassed that Chelsea was fat. No, that didn't make sense, Chelsea reasoned. Her mom was kind of fat too. Then Chelsea almost jumped out of bed. She had almost, almost let herself forget Henry Yurt's terrible idea. Pajama Day. Coming up on Friday. Chelsea sighed.

☙

✿

EMERGENCY SEWING SESSION

The BSG had to call an emergency sewing session in the Tower. Katani and Isabel had bought the striped material and gotten the pajamas cut out, but said no way would they be able to do all the work by Friday.

Avery dragged her feet as she carried a load of sewing supplies up the steps to the Tower. "Do I really have to sew?" she complained. "I seriously don't know what to do. I'll probably sew the bottoms up by mistake so we'll all end up with girly footsie pajamas instead of realistic prison uniforms."

"Relax, Ave," Katani replied. "It's really not that hard ... and it doesn't have to be perfect. You can always rip stitches out and start over."

One of the last-minute ideas was going to take time. Maeve looked in her father's movie books and found that prisoners back in the old prison movies, like the one with Humphrey Bogart, *Angels with Dirty Faces*, wore little caps to match their uniforms. "We have to have the caps," Maeve insisted. "They'll be too, too cool."

"Cha-ching," Katani said. "We won't have to buy more material, but we'll have to spend more time. We can put some felt in the hats to make them have some shape, and you, Charlotte and Avery, can hand sew them. Are you willing to do that?"

"What if I volunteer to be a go-fer?" Avery suggested. "I'll go-fer goldfish crackers. I'll go to the kitchen and make popcorn. I'll be in charge of keeping energy up and keeping Marty from helping. He probably needs a run. Are you running with him every morning, Charlotte?"

Exasperated, Charlotte said, "Avery, you know, even Marty likes to sleep in some days. You can miss a day of exercise and not fall apart. I try to take Marty for a walk in the park after school, but we've had all this extra work. It's like teachers can't stand us to miss a day or two, so they give us double homework before we leave."

"We can protest that, too. One of our signs on the back of the uniforms can say, NO MORE HOMEWORK. The trip is supposed to be part of our curriculum. I'll bet we have to write papers after we get back." Avery flopped down and did ten sit-ups, as if that would make her feel better about having to write a paper. Charlotte, Katani, Isabel, and Maeve groaned. No one could keep up with Avery. She had more energy than anyone they knew.

"What I did on my outdoor education vacation." Maeve giggled. "I'll make up a skit that shows some of our adventures. Or several skits. Wasn't there a dance in the sixties called 'The Swim'?" Maeve jumped up, popped on a CD, and started swaying and moving like a fish.

She puckered up her lips and made a slight popping sound, as if she was sucking air.

Soon all the girls were sucking air, making like goldfish, swaying at whatever task they were trying to do. The skit didn't last long, since neither Katani nor Isabel could sew a straight line while standing up and swimming.

"Is this right?" Maeve popped her finished convict hat on her red hair and struck a pose in which she was sad and peering through bars, longing for freedom.

"No, you look like a flight attendant." Charlotte said. "The hat goes on sideways." She slipped the hat off Maeve and turned it around.

"That's not nearly as cute." Maeve looked in the mirror and pouted.

"You're the one who said we have to be true to the old movies."

"Well, not completely true. Because one thing that was really gross is that people used to smoke in them all the time. Even fancy people. It's disgusting. I hate smoke." Maeve acted out a huge coughing fit for her friends.

"Yeah, it's like where did anyone get the idea that it's so cool to smoke? Let's all smoke and destroy our lungs. There's a great concept," Avery said sarcastically.

"You know," Isabel said conspiratorially. "My sister went out with this boy who smoked. He was really handsome and nice, but Elena Maria said that when she was near him she could smell the smoke. It made her nauseous. So she broke up with him."

"That's so sad," Maeve cried. "Why didn't she tell him to give up smoking if he was so cute?"

"She did tell him, but he couldn't give them up. He said he was addicted and he was only fifteen." Isabel sighed as she put the final touches on her hat.

"Oh," sighed Maeve, her romantic sensibilities dashed.

Charlotte didn't know how they got from Pajama Day to smoking, but Isabel's story reminded her of how she was never ever going to smoke in her life even if the coolest person in the whole world asked her to. The idea of breathing in smoke was really creepy. She shivered at the thought.

"What do you think Chelsea Briggs is going to wear?" asked Katani as she held her pj pants out in front of her.

"I know what she should wear," Maeve said excitedly. "She should go dressed like a queen. Chelsea would look great all big and beautiful and strong like no one would mess with her."

"That's a great idea, Maeve." Isabel jumped up. "Let's call her right now." Isabel was still feeling a little guilty about her cartoon. This, she thought, would help make it up to Chelsea.

Avery jumped up to get the phone book.

Charlotte and Katani looked at each other and shook their heads.

Katani spoke first. "Look. We don't really know Chelsea. I mean, what if Kiki called us up and said we should wear our mothers' pajamas?"

The girls all looked at each other and Maeve began to giggle. "You would not believe what my mother wears to bed in the winter ... old Mickey Mouse pjs with feet."

"I agree with Katani," Charlotte said, suddenly serious. "Chelsea might be mad. It would be like saying that we know what's good for her and we hardly even know her."

The girls agreed that they should drop the idea. But Maeve still insisted that her idea had been a good one.

"You know, in olden times when they didn't worship stick-thin women, Chelsea might have been the most popular."

The information that Maeve had stored in her head, gleaned from movies over the years, was certainly a mish-mash of colorful vocabulary but sometimes useful facts.

"Do you want to come over on Friday morning so we can get dressed here? We can go to school together and make a grand entrance."

"Great idea," Maeve said. "I've had a lot of freedom lately, but occasionally Mom remembers I exist for something besides getting Sam off to school."

Working together, they finished their pajamas just as Mr. Ramsey said he'd take everyone home. "Do I get a fashion show?"

"The girls are going to come over before school on Friday."

"I'll be sure to have plenty of film in the camera. I'm amazed at the things you girls think of to do."

"Oh, this wasn't our idea, Mr. Ramsey. It was part of

Henry Yurt's campaign promise. If he was elected he'd get us permission to come to school in our pajamas," Katani laughed. "I never would have thought that Grandma Ruby would approve of it, but sometimes she surprises me."

"You girls should all go to bed early tonight to start resting up for Lake Rescue. I'll drive you home now. And, Charlotte, your light better be out by the time I get back!"

Mr. Ramsey winked at Charlotte as they left.

"It will be out, Dad. I'm tired. But I want to send Sophie a quick email tonight. She's going to think I've forgotten her."

```
To: Sophie
From: Charlotte
Subject: Pajama Day.

Sophie¬ ma cherie¬
u will not believe that the entire 7th
grade is wearing pajamas 2 school! LOL
Forgive me for not writing so often¬ but
we have been sewing¬ shopping¬ and packing.
Yes¬ packing. The entire 7th grade leaves
on Monday 4 a week of outdoor education
at a place called Lake Rescue. We'll hike¬
canoe¬ climb ropes and mountains and hope
no one needs 2 be rescued. Long letter
when we return. I promise.
Still your l'amie pour toujours (always!)¬
Charlotte
```

CHAPTER 9

൙

PAJAMA PARTY

THE GIRLS were laughing so hard on Friday morning that Mr. Ramsey had trouble getting them to stand still so he could take photos.

Despite Katani's efforts, Avery's pants were too long, and she had to roll them over a couple of times. Everyone's outfit was large so they could wear the pajamas over their clothing. The girls had decided on stretch pants and tank tops so you could scarcely notice anything but the striped pajamas—and, of course, the black balloons on their black electric-tape chains. They'd had to run extra tape around their socks in order to get them to stay on.

Fortunately, it wasn't too cold, since no way could they wear coats. Off they went, down Corey Hill, left on Beacon, left on Harvard. They walked in a straight line, right hand on the right shoulder of the person in front, so they appeared to be chained together. They giggled and laughed, trying not to step on each other's balloons.

"Left, right, left, right." Avery counted the cadence for marching.

✿

Charlotte waved to Yuri, outside arranging the fruit for his grocery. He started to wave back, then froze, staring. She saw him shake his head. The puzzled look on his face as they marched by was so comical that the BSG got another huge fit of laughter. Every time they tried to stop laughing, Maeve would imitate Yuri's long face, and they would burst into giggles all over again.

As they walked along the route to school, people stared, some laughed, all stopped and looked. Charlotte just hoped that she wouldn't fall down, as her pj bottoms kept unrolling.

"This is so great," Avery said, giving Maeve a high five. "Just imagine what an entrance we're going to make at school."

"Looks like we're already a success," Charlotte said, trying to imagine doing this at any other school she had attended. Most schools abroad tended to be more formal, more serious than Abigail Adams Junior High. Not that studying and learning wasn't the top priority at Abigail Adams, but having fun at school was considered necessary to make the school experience complete. Charlotte loved that about America. People always tried to make things fun. It was very "jolly" as her friend Shadya from Tanzania used to say. Of course, fun at Abigail Adams Junior High probably had a lot to do with Mrs. Fields too. She seemed to be able to remember what it was like to be a teenager.

Eighth graders stopped and stared. One girl put her hands on her hips and said, "How juvenile. I'm so glad I'm in eighth grade."

"So are we!" Maeve giggled. "Promise me, BSG, that we won't get so stuck up next year that we'll act like that."

After a rousing "We promise!" came a chorus of "yes," "no way," and "juvenile forever."

The Yurtmeister was greeting people at the door. He

wore a nightshirt with red toy soldiers on a background of white. In his hand he held a candlestick. On his head, a nightcap with a red tassel.

"Wow, good competition. Congratulations, girls. You are contenders."

Henry had made sure there were prizes worth having for several categories. Most original. Cutest. Funniest. Even a consolation prize called "Best Try." He had told the girls one day at lunch that several businesses had given him gift certificates from their stores.

Riley Lee carried a homemade CD cover that said, "Bedtime Stories." He wore headphones, and Charlotte wondered what he was really listening to.

Nick Montoya and Sammy Andropovitch leaned on their lockers. Both looked pretty standard in blue sweats with wine-colored piping and old t-shirts.

The girls got their books from their lockers, then hooked back up to march into homeroom. Ms. Rodriguez shook her head, grinned from ear to ear, then clapped. "Good show. If you don't win a prize, I'll find one for you."

Charlotte was excited. She felt so lucky to be a part of the BSG.

"Make new friends, but keep the old. One is silver, the other gold." Charlotte didn't know where she had learned that little song, and why it should pop into her head at this moment, but her silver friends were fast becoming gold. And to her relief, that morning she'd found three emails waiting for her from Sophie, who was surely, even with so much distance between them, still a gold friend.

The signs on their backs were a little scratchy to lean against, but people had shouted "right on" and raised thumbs in agreement to escaping the classroom and homework.

❀

"OK, class," Ms. Rodriguez said. "You really are going to be set free from your usual school activities on Monday. Is everyone packed and ready to meet the bus here at 7 a.m.? I'm sure no one wants to be left behind. The outdoor education experience is going to be worth 25% of your physical education grade for this quarter. Your chaperones, Ms. Weston, Mr. Brown, and Ms. Franklin, will evaluate the participation of each student." Ms. R passed out sheets of paper.

"Remember, your number one assignment is to keep a journal. Here are some suggestions for journal starters, but mainly I want you to 'free write' each day about your experiences. Each day, write about someone you helped and someone who helped you. What you learned about working together. If you get to know someone new, write about that person. If you learn something you never knew about yourself, or if someone surprises you, write about that. Any questions?"

"We have to write in the journal every day?" Avery asked. "That's going to spoil the whole trip."

"Yes, every day or sometimes during the day when you get a free moment. Your experiences are going to be kickoffs for other writing assignments upon your return. In fact, we've asked the camp counselors to give you periods of free time."

"When?" Avery asked. "From 6 to 6:30 in the morning and 9:30 to 10:00 at night?" Avery pretended to yawn.

"That's when I usually have my bedtime story." Henry Yurt grinned at Avery.

"Maybe you get a bedtime story, Yurt, but I always study my football plays just before I go to sleep." Pete Wexler was the quarterback on the J.V. football team. "Whatever you read or study just before you go to sleep stays in your mind."

"That's when I study for tests." Betsy Fitzgerald was a straight A student. Maybe studying before bedtime was one of her trade secrets. "I might not have perfect penmanship if I'm writing in a canoe, Ms. Rodriguez," she added. "Will you take that into consideration?"

"I'm not going to be reading your journals, Betsy. So don't worry about how messy they are ... poems and doodles are fine. In addition to writing, you can draw or color. Take your colored pencils. Just record your thoughts and favorite images about the trip."

"I don't think that will be too hard, Ms. R," Dillon grinned, looking around for someone to point his finger at.

"Are you going to bring your teddy bear so you can sleep at night?" Avery joked.

"Maybe, and what about you? Need your blankie?" grinned Dillon. They high-fived each other.

"I see a competition brewing," Charlotte whispered to Maeve.

"You think they would have learned from the class election." Maeve whispered back as she grinned at Dillon.

Charlotte nodded. Things had gotten so heated between Katani and Avery when they both had run for class president.

Charlotte wondered if she should take her stuffed pig on the trip. But what if Truffles got lost or stolen? That would be so sad. She'd had Truffles for ages. Besides, if she brought him, she might get teased. Better to leave him at home with Marty and Dad. That was the safe move.

"OK, everyone. Listen up now." Ms. Rodriguez continued with her announcements. "Henry made a strong argument for a new category—creativity. So be sure to vote by noon, so we can announce all the winners."

"Can we vote for ourselves?" Joline asked, sitting up very straight at her desk.

Charlotte would never have had the nerve to wear a satin

nightshirt like Joline wore today. Even over shorts and a tank. Anna's was identical yellow. They had obviously gone out and bought them new.

"You'd better vote for yourself. No one else will." A boy's voice came from the back of the room, but when everyone turned around, the speaker remained straight-faced, and Charlotte, at least, didn't recognize his voice.

"OK, have fun today, and—"

"Write about Pajama Day in our journals?" Avery finished Ms. Rodriguez' sentence. "And the ghost that haunts Lake Rescue." The bell rang so Ms. R didn't hear the rest of Avery's words.

Ms. O'Reilly, their young social studies teacher, smiled as everyone filed into her class. "Where did you girls get your idea for today's costumes, Charlotte?"

"Maeve told us about some old prison movies and we saw the movie poster for *Oh, Brother, Where Art Thou?*"

"Did you know that movie was based on a book called *The Odyssey*? It's considered a classic."

No one raised a hand except Betsy. "It's by Homer. Will we read it this year?" she asked.

"No, not yet."

"Homer Simpson?" asked Henry Yurt. The whole class broke into hysteria.

"No, Henry, a different Homer ... he lived several thousand years ago in ancient Greece. Does anyone know what the word *odyssey* means?"

Charlotte had heard her father use the word. She took a wild guess.

"Does it mean a trip?"

"Yes, it does. A long, adventurous journey. Kind of like the one you're getting ready to make to Lake Rescue."

"I hope it won't be too adventurous," Maeve said. Charlotte knew she still wished she could stay home, even though the trip would have been spoiled without all the BSG.

"What are some examples you can think of in history that might be odysseys?" Ms. O'Reilly's sparkling green eyes encouraged someone to take a chance on answering her question. She made students want to have the answer to her questions, but she never put them down if they said something stupid.

Dillon took a chance. "Would the voyage of Christopher Columbus be considered an odyssey?"

"Certainly. I think the voyages of many curious explorers would qualify. The voyage of Lewis and Clark across the western half of the United States was an odyssey. And Powell's trip down the Colorado River when he had no idea what he'd find around the next bend was an odyssey too."

"What about Leif Eriksson and the Vikings?" offered Nick. A history buff, Nick was obsessed with the Vikings. To him they were the ultimate adventurers—sailing the seas in their small, sturdy ships.

"Yes, Nick. I would definitely think the Viking journeys would qualify as odysseys."

"What if I fly to Colorado next summer to visit my dad?" Avery asked. "Is that an odyssey?"

"I don't think so, Avery." Billy Trentini grinned at Avery. "You get on a plane in Boston, you drink a Coke, you get off in Denver?"

"Maybe by the time you came home, Avery, you'd have had some adventures and the trip would qualify. But as a rule, I think the word suggests a long, sometimes frightening, often difficult journey in which you learn some things about a new world and yourself. I'm looking in my dictionary." Ms. O'Reilly thumbed through a fat, well-worn book. "Ah, here it is. The words hardship, wandering and adventurous are mentioned."

Katani grimaced. "That figures. Since I have to go to Lake Rescue, there will definitely be hardship involved." Katani slapped high fives with Maeve and Isabel. All three of them had tried but failed to get out of the outdoor education trip.

"Good. We'll talk more about this when you return. Be sure—"

The entire class had the words memorized. "To write down what happens all week."

By noon, when prizes were announced, Billy and Josh Trentini had popped all the girls' "ball and chain" balloons, and they had taken the tape off their socks.

"You know," Avery said, "these pajamas are comfortable. Maybe we can wear them all the time. Except when I'm playing soccer, of course."

"They're warm and cozy, too," Isabel said. "I've had trouble not falling asleep in class."

"There's Chelsea." Maeve avoided pointing, but she nodded several tables over. "Hey, those don't look like pjs."

Chelsea Briggs wore sweatpants and a football t-shirt with a number, which probably belonged to her brother.

"They are." Isabel made her purple Jell-O quiver every time she took a bite. "I asked her. She said that's really what she sleeps in every night. That's one of her brother's old shirts. Her brother Ben is some famous football player at the high school."

"All right, attention all you pajamaheads." Henry Yurt tossed his tasseled hat out of his eyes and stood in front of the seventh-grade tables. "What you've waited for all morning. The awards!"

All the BSG pretended they didn't care if they won anything, but there was lots of punching and giggling going on around them.

"Nice try." Henry waved a piece of paper. "Nick and Sammy get a gift certificate to Filene's Basement 'cause they really need some new pjs. You dudes get the 'Need Help' award. I think the Basement has some."

"Or give the gift certificate to someone else." Maeve raised her eyebrows and pretended she didn't mean herself. The Basement was her favorite place to shop.

"Prettiest. Who else? Joline Kaminsky and Anna McMasters. Gift certificates to Burger Barn."

Had Henry done that on purpose? Obviously Joline and Anna thought he had. They were sitting at the table behind the BSG so their reaction was easily overheard.

"Burger Barn! We'd never eat there. Their hamburgers have about a thousand calories apiece." Joline was outraged at their prize.

"Hey, I love those burgers," piped up Avery.

"Well, you take the ticket then," Joline answered sarcastically.

"Great," Avery held out her hand, but Joline put her nose in the air and walked away.

"Hey, let's trade prizes with Nick and Sammy ... sometimes you can find some cool things there," Anna said, staring straight at Maeve.

"Good luck," Maeve whispered.

"Most creative." Henry waved the last gift certificate. "Big surprise. The award goes to the jailbirds, Charlotte, Avery, Maeve, Katani, and Isabel. An evening of bowling at Stardust Lanes."

"Bowling?" Maeve's face fell as fast as it had lit up.

Avery jumped up. "I love bowling—it's so fun. You'll see. We'll have a great time."

Maeve had to admit, doing anything with Avery was fun. She had so much enthusiasm.

The BSG marched up in their line to get the prize. Applause and cheering filled the lunchroom.

"No more school." "Escape this place." "No homework."

"Did we win because of the costumes or the signs?" Katani whispered.

"Doesn't matter. We had fun. Remember the BSG oath. One of our most important rules is to have as much fun as we can." As Minister of Fun, Romance, and Entertainment, Maeve took her position *really* seriously.

Charlotte had to admit that she had never had so much fun at any of her other schools as she was having at Abigail Adams Junior High. Of course, she had worked really hard too. Mrs. Fields made sure that the Abigail Adams school was one of the top achieving in Massachusetts. That's probably why she let kids have fun. She didn't want the students getting too stressed out, figured Charlotte. And now, they had something out of the ordinary to look forward to ... for better or worse. Four days in the New Hampshire woods. Charlotte couldn't wait.

"Let's take our new pajamas to camp," Charlotte suggested.

"Why not? Like I said, they're warm." Isabel agreed.

"Let's leave the signs behind. But I predict that in one day, we might want to escape," Maeve said.

"I'll hitchhike home with you," Katani and Isabel said at the same time.

"Are we the only two looking forward to Lake Rescue, Avery?" Charlotte asked, taking her lunch tray to turn in.

"Looks that way, Char. But just wait. I predict nothing but total fun on this next adventure. Once we all get there it will be Beacon Street Girls rule!" Avery slapped hands with Charlotte and the other three joined in, not even knowing why. Avery and Charlotte were sure that the next week would go down in BSG history—their excitement was contagious.

CHAPTER 10

❧

FIRST-NIGHT JITTERS

"OH, 7 a.m. IS TOO EARLY for anything, especially to be ready to get on a bus and drive forever." Maeve groaned and dragged her stuff toward the bus.

Avery turned a cartwheel in the school driveway. "We had to leave early," she said from her upside-down position, "so we don't miss any lake time," she added breathlessly.

"I looked on the map," Charlotte said. "It's practically next door. And Dad and I looked at the star charts. We think the stars will be almost same as in Boston."

"Are we there yet?" Maeve pushed a suitcase and two backpacks into the back of the bus.

"Hey, girl, you cheated." Katani put her hands on her hips. "You can only bring one small suitcase, and one backpack or overnight case."

"Whoever made that rule should have come and helped me pack." Maeve yawned.

"We're only going to be there for four days." Avery had given up on the cartwheels and was now dribbling a basketball around the driveway. It was like she couldn't sit still for one minute she was so excited.

"That's what I mean. We're going to be there four days." Maeve climbed onto the bus and looked for a window seat.

"We're uneven." Avery followed Maeve onto the bus, spinning the basketball on one finger. The bus driver said that she had to leave it at the front of the bus for safety. Disappointed, Avery looked around for empty seats. "Someone has to sit by themselves."

"No way." Nick Montoya walked up.

Charlotte took the window seat behind Katani and Maeve, and Nick slid in beside her. Out of the corner of her eye, she saw Chelsea Briggs in the back fooling with a camera. Charlotte had noticed Chelsea taking photographs earlier.

"Hey, where's Riley?" Maeve wondered out loud. "He was supposed to bring me a mix CD to listen to on the bus."

Mrs. Fields poked her head in through the front door as she answered Maeve's question.

"Unfortunately, Riley Lee is sick ... with a bad cold and fever. His mother called me this morning. So, I am afraid Riley won't be able to join us at Lake Rescue."

"Oh," was all Maeve said. But she was surprised at how disappointed she felt. She and Riley had become friends when they worked together on a song for the last school dance, and Maeve had to admit he was pretty cute ... in that rock star grunge sort of way.

"Too bad," Dillon piped in sarcastically, clearly jealous at the dispirited look on Maeve's face. Dillon still had a crush on Maeve and didn't quite know what to do about it. There was just something about the lively redhead that made his heart skip a beat.

Mrs. Fields wasn't going, of course, but she would never miss the send-off. She asked everyone to get settled so that she could make a few announcements.

She pointed to Chelsea in the back of the bus. "Chelsea Briggs is our official photographer for the trip. If any of you see something worth a photograph, I'm sure Chelsea would be open to your suggestions."

Immediately some kids struck poses for Chelsea.

"Of course, anyone hogging the camera will be discovered when they're put on the computer screen." After twenty years of being a junior high principal, Katani's grandmother had seen every junior high trick in the book. "Just go about your business. I have instructed Chelsea to try and make sure that she captures candids of everyone."

"Smile, you're on candid camera." Avery held her chocolate-covered breakfast bar as if it were a camera and she was clicking off photos. She aimed it right at Charlotte and Nick. Secretly, Charlotte wished it were a camera.

"Save your energy for the ropes course," Billy Trentini said to Avery after Mrs. Fields left to talk to the other bus.

"I'll bet you I can do it faster than you any day of the week," Avery challenged.

"What do I win?" Billy asked. "How about your dessert every night we're on the trip?"

Avery hesitated. But just for a moment. "Done. I'd love two desserts every night." She bounced a high five off Billy's outstretched hand.

"Billy is going to hate going without dessert," Charlotte whispered to Nick. They both laughed. Billy Trentini was famous for his lunches ... a couple of sandwiches, soup, and his all-time favorite cookies—chocolate chip oatmeal raisin. Though no one could ever figure out where it all went on Skinny Billy.

CR

Charlotte felt a little funny sitting beside Nick for the entire trip, but on the other hand, she liked being there too. Nick was really nice and he liked adventures. They talked about Lake Rescue and what might happen, until Maeve began to sing an old kindergarten song. Only being Maeve, she'd added a catchy reggae beat.

"The people on the bus go round and round, yeah, round and round, yeah, up and down. The people on the bus go round and round, all about the town." Nick began to sing, too. Charlotte didn't have much of a singing voice, but she joined in anyway and soon everybody on the bus followed. She thought that they all could have been in Jamaica cruising along the beach.

Charlotte remembered loving this song. She searched for a memory of her mother singing it to her. Sometimes she didn't know when memories and imagination got blurred. Whether something she wished to remember so badly had actually happened, or whether she had wished it into seeming real. She was sure that she remembered her mother reading to her all the time. She must have sung to her, too. Charlotte had learned the bus song somewhere.

"A penny?" Nick said, and Charlotte realized the singing had stopped.

"What?"

"Penny for your thoughts. My grandmother used to say that to me, and I wouldn't tell her what I was thinking about until she actually *gave* me a penny," he grinned.

"Oh, I was just thinking about my mother."

"Must be hard. I can't imagine my mother not being in the bakery every day, cooking up a storm."

"What's your favorite ... in the bakery?" asked Charlotte.

"I can't resist my mother's butterscotch cookies. Package

them with a latte and I am one happy customer." Nick sighed with satisfaction.

"Your parents let you drink coffee?"

"Yeah, it's kind of a Latin thing."

Nick couldn't help but be a nice guy coming from his family. Every time you went into Montoya's you got a real friendly hello from his mom and dad, or his sister Fabiana.

Charlotte hoped that somewhere her mother was proud of her, knew that she was OK, and that her daughter had great friends, lived in a cool yellow Victorian house with a funny little dog, and had been on adventures all over the world with her father. Charlotte thought it would be so wonderful if her mother knew all of that.

Even with a pit stop they were scheduled to arrive at Lake Rescue way before noon. Looking at the map with her father, Charlotte realized that where they were going in New Hampshire was just a couple hours' drive from Boston. Perhaps she and her father would have more time to explore next summer, especially if he didn't teach summer school.

With everyone quiet and half awake, Avery entertained those close to her, not with the ghost story her brother had told her about the camp, but with another she'd made up that she liked better.

"Years ago, when the camp had just opened, a young girl disappeared while on a cross-country hike. Although her friends and all the camp counselors looked and looked, Marie Darling was never found. The popular theory was that she wandered away from the other hikers and drowned in one of the many lakes there. Searchers dragged the lakes, looking for her body, but they never found one clue: a shoe, a piece of clothing, nothing."

Avery paused for effect. She knew how to tell a story.

"Now, at certain times of the day, early morning, late at night, and especially on foggy or rainy days, she walks the camp, searching for her friends. Many have heard her cry, many have continued to look for her, but still no clues. Just her soft sobbing or occasionally a scream echoes through the woods."

Everyone fell silent, but then Maeve giggled. "Good story, Avery. I hope we hear her."

"I'd just as soon not." Isabel yawned. She had dozed off until Avery started talking.

They turned onto a narrow road where an old wooden sign, needing paint, read LAKE RESCUE. Woods closed in around them, even brushing the sides of the bus at times. The bus bumped and bounced on the old dirt road. One huge pothole sent Avery flying to the ceiling. "Woo, hoo" she yelled as everyone on the bus cheered.

"What do you want to bet this isn't a five-star campground?" Katani said. "If I hadn't seen the sign, I'd say we were lost."

"If we are, the other bus is, too." Avery kneeled in her seat and looked out the back windows. "Think of having to haunt this place for fifty years. No grocery store, no baseball games, and no pizza."

Everyone on the bus was talking as the bus pulled up in front of what had to be the main building. People pushed and shoved, eager to stretch their legs and smell the pine trees. They were handed blank name tags and pens as they got off and asked to fill in the name tags and put them on.

"Welcome, welcome, campers." A tall, pretty, friendly-looking woman with a short afro greeted them. Five other counselors stood in a line beside her.

"Whoa," Maeve whispered, pointing to one of the male

counselors. "That guy is so cute. I hope we're in his group!"

Charlotte quickly grabbed Maeve's arm. "Maeve, he can see you pointing at him," she whispered back, blushing.

"My name is Jody," the woman announced. "I'm the head counselor at Lake Rescue. And this is Nash, Kim, John, Mia, and Terry, your other counselors. We will be leading your hikes and teaching you about the wildlife at the camp. Oh, and I'm also one of the two cooks—a very important position."

"Who is the other cook?" somebody shouted out.

"One of you campers," came the snappy answer.

Jody continued on as if the interruption had been a pesky mosquito needing to be brushed away. "As you will find out, everyone pitches in here.

Everyone works." She paused to let that word sink in.

"I don't do windows," a voice from the back of the crowd spoke up.

Jody grinned. "None of us does windows very often, but if you want to eat, you'll get your chores for the day done on time.

"If I had to say what was the foremost philosophy for Lake Rescue, it would be learning to get along together. We work together. We play together. We learn together."

"Do we dance together?" Another unidentified male voice blurted out.

Without missing a beat, Jody continued.

"Only if you are good. Want to come up and audition?"

A few snickers and then silence from the peanut gallery. Jody was tough; nothing fazed her. And she was quick-witted. Katani liked that in a camp leader.

But, Jody sounded more like a Marine drill sergeant the longer she talked. Even her stance imitated that of someone addressing new recruits. "Any questions?"

"Can we choose bunk mates?" Betsy asked the question that Charlotte would have expected from Joline or Anna.

"In a word, no. At Lake Rescue we like you to get to know new people ... learn to accept other people ... other perspectives different from your own. You may end up with a group of people who are almost total strangers to you at school. But, you may be surprised. You might even go home with new friends."

The BSG looked at each other. No way. No matter who they had to pair off with here at camp, they would go home the same best friends they had been since school started. Well, almost since school started. Charlotte liked meeting new people, and she had met so many interesting ones in her travels. But there was something special to her about being a Beacon Street Girl. Would new friends change their special relationship? She hoped not. She saw Isabel smile over at her and she felt better. Isabel had joined the BSG after Charlotte, and the group had survived.

"You will be engaging in activities that will help you build bonds with new people. You'll be learning to challenge yourself, help others with their own challenges. All of you will have brought some level of skills with you, but you will leave with many more. I think you'll be impressed with what you can do when you try and when other people support your efforts.

"We'll be outside most of the time. We hope you nature-deprived city kids will also leave with a new respect for your environment. If you have always lived in a city, you will be surprised at our rich and fascinating outdoor world—how many creatures live here, how to get along with and live side by side with them."

"Lions and tigers and bears, oh my ..." Dillon had sneaked up behind Maeve and whispered the warning. She giggled and shoved him away.

"Now, the first thing we have to do is assign you to teams. Please line up. With this many people, maybe two or three lines. We'll help you divide up."

The BSG lined up together, of course, which turned out to be the wrong thing to do. Jody and the other counselors made them count off.

One, two, three, four. When people caught on and started moving around, they were caught and put back to where they first stood.

"Number ones are the blue team." Jody separated them out. Charlotte, Isabel, Joline, Betsy, Sammy, and Nick were all number ones. "You will be working with John." Jody grabbed Anna as she tried to trade with Sammy, who was perfectly willing to get off a mostly all-girls team. "No trading. I'm almost ready to hand out demerits, which translates to extra kitchen duty. What are your names? Josh and Pete—you are blue teamers."

Charlotte looked at Isabel and shrugged. At least the two of them were still together. But how did the three other BSG get on the same team? Avery just smiled and waved, looking like the cat that swallowed the canary.

"Blue team, start sweeping bunk rooms." Jody hurried the first group away. Charlotte turned and waved at the rest of the BSG.

"You mean no one has cleaned, knowing we were coming?" Sammy complained. John handed Charlotte a broom, smiled, and made a sweeping motion.

"You are the green team," Jody said, pointing to Maeve, Avery, Katani, Anna, Dillon, Billy, Henry, Kiki, and Chelsea. "Your group is bigger because you're the fire builders. Tonight you're in charge of building a fire and cooking dinner. That takes some prep work. And we eat early here at Lake Rescue. Go drop your bags off in your cabins, and meet back here. Just follow the path." She clapped her hands. "Hop to it." Jody pointed toward the fire pits and the dining hall.

"I'm on the green team," Henry Yurt said, carrying his bags to his bunk. "How totally logical, since I ran the Green Food campaign for class president."

"We'll all be green if we have to eat something you've cooked, Yurt," Dillon said, following him.

"Ditto that." Maeve hurried behind the two boys, carrying her bags. "I've never cooked on a campfire, but I've had to help out at home more lately. We'll probably just throw

✿

everything in one pot and set it on the fire. How hard could that be?"

☙

Everyone was back in a flash. No one wanted to keep Jody waiting.

Meanwhile, a thin fog that had crept in gave the campground an eerie feel. Some of the campers looked knowingly at each other. As the minutes passed, the fog thickened and things began to feel damp.

Jody gave a short explanation of how to look for the right kind of kindling and then sent them off.

Katani shivered as she picked up kindling. She hoped that it wasn't going to rain. Her sisters' warning that rain made Lake Rescue "sheer misery" had stuck in her mind.

When the gatherers returned, it soon became apparent that the mist and fog had dampened the wood they'd picked up. Starting the fire was going to be difficult. Jody demonstrated a few safety precautions, and showed them how to build a little nest of twigs to get things started. Then she stood back.

"Isn't anybody a Boy Scout?" Dillon asked, singeing his fingers on another match that refused to get the fire started.

"Don't look at me," Anna said. She was sitting on a log in the fire circle, watching.

"Good grief." Avery ripped off three name tags, wadded them in a ball, and put more small sticks in a tent over the paper. "Now, give me a match." She took the book of matches, struck one, held it to the paper, and blew very slightly. Then stepped back. Within a few seconds, a cheery flame leaped a couple of inches high. "Now, let's put a few logs on the fire."

"I might have known you could start a fire, Avery." Maeve laughed. "Score one for girl power."

Jody gave her an enthusiastic thumbs up.

Chelsea snapped a photo of them, blowing, adding small sticks, keeping the flames building until they could tent logs around the fire pit.

Kiki stepped up to the group and looked at Chelsea. "I guess Jody assigned you to cooking, Chelsea." Then she paused and added, "It's kind of obvious why."

Maeve sighed inwardly. Kiki Underwood, true to her name, was famous for her sneak attacks.

"Take it back, Kiki," Katani, defender of the underdog, said. "Leave Chelsea alone."

"*Excuse* me." Kiki shook her head and put her hands on her hips. "Chill out, Summers—this is none of your business."

Chelsea stepped in front of her. "I can take care of myself."

"This is ridiculous," said Maeve, and she took Katani's arm and pulled her away from both Chelsea and Kiki. She knew Katani always sided with the underdog, and she liked helping people, but they didn't need a full-out war on their first day at camp.

"Chelsea, come on. Leave Kiki to her own happy self." Maeve urged.

Neither girl budged. The other campers were all waiting to see what happened next.

Suddenly Jody appeared. "Why is everybody standing around? Get busy. Chelsea, you're on kitchen duty. Meet me in the kitchen. I'll show you tonight's menu and where things are located. Go along now," she directed firmly.

Chelsea stared at Kiki, her eyes flashing fireworks. Reluctantly, she turned and headed toward the kitchen. Maeve and Katani looked at each other with relief and went back to warm themselves at the fire.

Jody took an unrepentant Kiki firmly by the arm and walked a short distance away from the fire. No one could hear what she was saying. But everyone could see the flush on Kiki's face.

Katani looked at Maeve. "Kiki Underwood needs a major attitude adjustment. She acts like a bully."

"I couldn't agree more," said Maeve. "I just don't get why she has to be so insulting all the time. I mean, it's like what Mrs. Weiss always says, "Live and let live." Katani nodded in agreement. The owner of Irving's Toy and Card shop always had the best advice. Simple and easy to follow. She also had great toys, comic books, and candy. It was a winning combination for the students at Abigail Adams.

"We've got a lot of work to do," Jody said as she entered the kitchen.

Chelsea, who was leaning against the long metal table, hoped Jody had not come down too hard on Kiki. She didn't want an enemy at camp.

Chelsea had been contemplating her showdown with Kiki. She knew that she never would have done anything to Kiki, but she was surprised at how angry she had felt toward her, and also how strange it had felt for Katani to actually stand up for her.

Chelsea said nothing as she waited for more directions from Jody. The counselor motioned for her to pick up a big bag of potatoes and bring it to the table.

"How are you doing?" Jody asked, getting down pots and pans and opening the sack of potatoes.

"What?" Chelsea knew what Jody meant, but she didn't feel like talking to some stranger about the way Kiki Underwood, Ms. Size 1 Mean Girl, had spoken to her. Maybe if she feigned non-interest, Jody would change the subject. "Kiki was not very nice to you out there."

No such luck, Chelsea shrugged. "I can handle it ... Kiki's a lightweight." Good joke, thought Chelsea. She wondered if the counselor would get it.

Jody smiled but kept on with her "agenda."

"You know, the name-calling is unacceptable. It's really harassment, even if there is a ring of truth in it." Chelsea was suddenly confused. Was Jody talking about her or Kiki?

"I think I know how you handle situations like that." There was a long pause. Chelsea stopped breathing. "You eat," Jody added.

Here it comes, thought Chelsea. You would be such a pretty girl if you lost weight. Why don't you try eating healthier and exercising more and then life would be perfect, blah, blah, blah.

"I did the same thing. When I was your age, I weighed even more than you do."

This was new. "You did?" Chelsea found she was curious in spite of herself. Jody looked really fit. She wasn't thin, but she looked pretty good.

"Yeah, I was a really overweight kid, and got bullied — people called me names all the time. But then I went off to this outdoor camp ... one much tougher than this one. And it got me started in a new direction with my weight and with myself. If you ever want to talk about it sometime, I'm around.

"Now, camper, pass me another bag of potatoes, will you, and grab one of those peelers. I could use some help." She grinned at Chelsea.

"I'm the trip photographer," Chelsea said. "I probably won't have a lot of time to talk."

She grabbed a potato and started peeling. Real fun, she

fumed. I get to peel potatoes and talk about how much I weigh. Maybe if she stopped talking, the counselor would just change the subject. But then, after a few minutes, it occurred to her that if she talked with Jody, maybe she could get out of some of the hikes or the rope climbing. Might be worth a try, she thought.

And Jody wasn't being pushy anyway. She didn't seem like some do-gooder, nosy type.

"Sometime I'll tell you how I went from being a heavy, out-of-shape weakling to this wilderness goddess you see standing before you." Jody lifted up her arms and made a muscle. Chelsea couldn't help but laugh. Jody made the weight issue seem manageable.

"But now we'd better go get dinner started. Help me carry some of these things and I'll send some other kids in to help you finish peeling."

In a few minutes, Nash walked back in with a group of kids. Soon lots of hands got busy peeling, chopping, and throwing ingredients into a big pot for the famous Lake Rescue campfire stew. The smell of braising meat, then onions, and finally the herbs made the green team hope they could be first in line for their own cooking.

Maeve and Katani made buttered bread sandwiches and cut them across into triangles. Both girls laughed as they raced to see which one of them could make the most sandwiches in one minute. S'mores, the favorite BSG sleepover dessert, were also on the menu tonight.

After everyone settled down on the ground or a rock with a plateful of food, the conversations became quieter. Having to work for their food had made them hungry, and everyone concentrated on the stew for a few minutes.

Suddenly, something mushy hit the back of Avery's head.

As she turned around, another ball of stew-soaked bread sailed right into her bowl.

"Heyyy!" she yelled. "Who did that?"

She caught Josh giving his brother Billy a low five.

Avery balled up a piece of her own bread, dunked it in her stew, and before Billy knew what was coming, hit him squarely in the forehead with the gooey mess. Luckily, Chelsea had her camera ready. The picture of a shocked Billy with goop on his face would be a winner.

That was all it took. One side of the campfire against the other, the food began to fly. Henry Yurt picked up a carrot that hadn't been chopped and ran in circles, shouting, "I have a carrot, and I'm not afraid to use it!"

Jody jumped up and blew her whistle. "Enough! If I get hit with a piece of somebody's chewed-up dinner, I will NOT be a happy camper! Besides, you're wasting good food, which is just plain wrong. Pick up everything and put it in the trash … NOW. We don't want any creatures visiting us in the middle of the night because you were all acting like a bunch of hyenas."

Chelsea thought she saw a hint of a smile on Jody's face, even though she was acting really strict. Something told her this wasn't the first food fight that had happened at Lake Rescue … and it wouldn't be the last.

The night air grew even more foggy. Everyone was eager to huddle around the fire after dinner.

Avery spoke, breaking the unusual silence. "Remember, the ghost really likes foggy evenings. Tonight looks perfect."

"Avery!" Isabel scolded. "Did you have to spoil my dinner?"

Ooo,oooo,ooo,oooo,ooo,oooo,ooo,oooo.

A single, throbbing note floated through the fog, across

the campground, then became a trembling wail.

"OMG! What's that?" Charlotte was sitting next to Nick and didn't think twice about grabbing hold of his arm.

"Who else?" Avery said. "It's Marie Darling calling us to come and find her. Any volunteers for a midnight hike?"

PART TWO

MOUNTAINS TO CLIMB

CHAPTER 11

ߏ

UNDERFABULOUS

"YOU'RE KIDDING, right?" Isabel hugged her knees tighter. "Please, tell me Avery is kidding." She glanced over at Jody, then at the other counselors, all huddled around the fire.

"It sounded like a ghost, a real ghost." Maeve looked scared. Charlotte couldn't tell if Maeve was acting or she really was afraid.

Jody laughed. "That, all you nature-deprived city kids, is a loon. These birds live on the lakes and ponds all around Lake Rescue. They are known for their haunting cry."

"A real bird made that noise?" Chelsea looked skeptical.

"Creepy, isn't it?" John, the counselor, joined in on the conversation. "Quite a few mysterious legends have grown up around the loon. The Cree Indians believed the loon's strange and eerie cry was that of a dead warrior forbidden entry into heaven." You could hear a pin drop around the campfire.

Then Nash issued a soft warning. "The Chippewa Indians believed the loon's cry was an augury of death."

Suddenly, the night filled with the lonely cry of the loon. There were gasps ... then giggles from the campers.

❁

Maeve grabbed Katani's hand.

Charlotte had to admit, the timing of the loon's cry was unnerving. But the writer in her just had to know. "What does augury mean?"

"A prediction, an omen, or a warning. The Chippewa thought the loon might be predicting someone's death."

"You mean one of us is going to die out here?" Dillon asked. No one could tell if he was teasing or serious.

Nash opened his mouth to answer but Avery jumped to her feet before he could say a word.

"OK, OK, all you Abigail Adams campers, story hour is over." Avery was either getting scared herself, or she really was tired for a change.

"Great idea," echoed Jody. "Now, let's all get a move on it. We've got a lot to do tomorrow." She motioned for all the campers to head back to their respective bunks.

All the BSG jumped up. They were ready to put their heads on the pillow and sleep for twelve hours. Last week had been so busy.

"I hate it that we aren't all in a cabin together." Katani took Maeve's arm. "But, at least, you and I are together."

"I'm in the bunk with you and Isabel, Char. Cool, huh!" Avery high-fived her friend. "Yeah, they put some of us greenies in with some of you bluies. Must be some kind of social experiment, like the Star-Belly Sneetches from Dr. Seuss." Avery laughed heartily at her own joke.

"Did you see Anna try to change teams and cabins?" Maeve laughed. "She's so mad she's stuck with us. Such a tragedy to have to sleep in the same bunk as Katani and me."

"Or—" Avery didn't get to finish her sentence.

"Be nice, Avery. We're here to work together." Katani laughed.

"Give me a break, Kgirl. I was going to say that Anna is an awesome athlete," Avery blurted. "I'd choose her for my team."

Avery categorized people by athlete/nonathlete. That would be obnoxious, thought Charlotte, if Avery wasn't so willing to play sports with anyone who felt like playing.

"I don't know, Ave," Katani said, shaking her head. "I just don't have a lot of trust where the Queens of Mean are concerned. You remember the talent show?"

Avery shrugged her shoulders. "You've got a point. But I have to let stuff like that go when I'm playing sports. I really like to win, so I'd still have to go for Anna for my team."

"Over me, Ave?" Katani asked, her hands planted on her hips. There was a twinkle in her eye, however. Katani had no pretensions regarding her own athletic abilities.

Maeve shook out her ponytail. "Can we please just go to bed now? I'm so tired and I know I'm going to have to make like a wilderness woman tomorrow."

Avery picked up a pine cone and threw it toward Maeve. "Catch this, 'Maeve of the Jungle.'"

To everyone's surprise Maeve caught the cone with one hand. The look on her face was one of such shock that the BSG began to laugh hysterically. With that Maeve threw open her arms dramatically and pleaded, "Group hug!"

The BSG rushed together and shared an enthusiastic Hollywood-style hug as if they wouldn't see each other again for the entire week.

Once inside their cabins, the girls remembered that Lake Rescue was no plush Hollywood spa. While the bunks were relatively neat, grass sprouted up in between the cabin's floor cracks. There were spider webs in the top corners of the room, and dust bunnies everywhere. "Somebody must have forgotten to sweep this cabin," said Isabel, a hint of annoyance in her voice.

Luckily, there were no spiders—at least not crawling around in plain view. However, if you blew into the air, the dust bunnies rose from everywhere and floated in front of your face. This was definitely roughing it.

But Charlotte was way too tired to care what her bunk looked like. A sleeping bag on top of rocks would look good right now, she sighed as she tossed her bag onto one of the lower bunks. Barely awake, she foraged in her backpack for her prison-striped pajamas and tugged them on. Her eyes were almost closing as she brushed her teeth. She felt oddly comforted by the sound of raindrops on the old wooden roof. It made for good sleeping, Charlotte thought dreamily.

છ

The next morning, sun streamed into the dusty cabin windows. Everyone began to stir. As Charlotte sat up to stretch, she noticed that Avery, who had bunked across from her, was already gone. But she had propped Happy Lucky Thingy against her pillow to remind herself of Marty. Avery must be at cooking duty, remembered Charlotte.

"I don't know if I'm more hungry or more tired." Isabel rubbed her eyes. "At least we don't have to get up and start a fire and cook bear."

"Bear?" Charlotte laughed. "For breakfast?"

"Some people still eat bear," Katani insisted as she poked her head in the cabin door.

"I'm sure bears are tasty when you are in the Alaskan wilderness and you have run out of mac and cheese, but otherwise, I'll pass." Charlotte shuddered. "Besides, bears have a right to wander around the forest and eat berries and vermin and fish, without worrying about someone looking to eat them for breakfast."

"You've been reading again, Charlotte," Isabel teased.

Charlotte nodded. "I couldn't help myself. I wanted to know what bears ate."

"Did you hear that loon at dawn?" a girl named Tanya asked.

Charlotte shook her head slowly.

"That one bird went on and on with that spooky cry. It almost sounded like a moan. Don't tell me you didn't hear it." Tanya looked incredulous. "It woke me up really early. Those birds were talkin' up a storm."

"I've learned to sleep almost anywhere." Charlotte dragged her bag into the small bathroom, took out her face towel, and laughed when she looked at it. Did loons steal towels? She soaked it in cold water and pressed it to her face. The shock of the cold helped a little. She was so tired. A thought that maybe the outdoor trip was going to require a little more energy than she originally planned whizzed through her brain.

Suddenly, there was knocking at the door. Charlotte poked her head out. She was surprised to see four girls impatiently standing in line with their towels and cosmetic bags.

"Sorry, I'll be out in a minute," Charlotte said with a smile, and closed the door again. She needed to finish brushing her teeth. Exactly one minute later, there were two sets of fists banging on the door. "Come on, let us in!"

Charlotte swung the door open and hurried out. "Sheesh," she muttered to Isabel.

Isabel laughed. "You don't have any *sisters*. Pounding on the door is an everyday occurrence when a group of girls shares a bathroom."

Much of the time Charlotte wished she had brothers and

sisters, but she suddenly realized there were some great perks to being an only child.

Charlotte and Isabel were among the last to arrive for breakfast.

"Did you think we were going to bring you breakfast in bed?" Avery laughed when she looked at Charlotte and Isabel. "Here! Have some cocoa. It's really, really good. Tastes homemade. Not that nasty stuff that tastes like you are drinking chemicals. No, if I'm gonna drink cocoa, give me the real deal—chocolate, caffeine, guaranteed to wake you up and get you really ready to roll."

With that Avery stood up on her chair and waved her arms back and forth rhythmically like she was at a rock concert. The whole dining room burst into clapping, except for the girls at Anna's and Kiki's table. Anna rolled her eyes. "Avery Madden is so immature," said Kiki. Anna and Joline nodded in agreement. Avery overheard her and stuck out her tongue at Kiki. She kept dancing until Jody told her to stop standing on her chair.

"Hey, Avery!" Billy Trentini shouted.

"You better give me some of that cocoa," Isabel said.

Charlotte warmed her hands around her own cup. The air was damp and nippy, but not really cold. Her woolly fleece jacket felt good for this early. Once the sun was out, she could probably change to a light jacket—not her lucky writing jacket, though. She had backed out on packing that at the last minute. Too risky. She wanted that jacket to last a lifetime. It had been her mother's and she hoped to wear it until it was as worn as her favorite stuffed, plush pig, Truffles. Maybe, if she was extra careful she could pass the jacket on to her own daughter someday.

Right then, Nick Montoya interrupted her reverie by handing her a plate of bacon, toast, and scrambled eggs. "Room service, just this once," he said and sat down at the table. "Did you dudes sleep OK? I managed to sneeze most of the night myself."

Charlotte laughed. Nick was so funny sometimes. "I was so tired I went to sleep the minute I crashed onto that bed. If you can call it a bed."

"No kidding." Nick nodded in agreement. "That creaky, metal-framed cot is definitely not something you would find at the Ritz," he said, crunching on a piece of bacon.

"Yeah, it was about as comfortable as sleeping on rocks," Charlotte said in between bites of toast.

"Well, you better finish your green eggs and ham," Nick smiled at Charlotte. "In exactly half an hour, we're going to be climbing *the wall*."

Charlotte looked up from her bacon. "You mean a real wall ... or a climbing wall?" She liked to hike but the idea of hanging upside down from a harness was a little daunting.

"Looks pretty real to me," Nick answered as he leaned back in his chair. "Dillon and I went for a walk this morning. This place is pretty wild. We saw the birds that make that spooky sound. They're pretty cool. You should see them dive for fish. They can stay down there for a really long time."

Charlotte vowed to get up early the rest of the week. She didn't want to miss a minute of what Lake Rescue had to offer.

Each camper was required to wash his or her tin plate and fork. But a whole team was assigned to kitchen cleanup. Charlotte was relieved it wasn't one of her jobs this morning.

Jody motioned for the green and blue teams to line up. The other teams had followed Mia to the lake. Jody handed out new name tags to everyone, explaining that there were only six counselors and a whole lot of campers. Katani whispered to Maeve, "We should draw flowers and pine cones on these tags. These are so boring looking."

Maeve agreed, and they both decided that they would decorate theirs when they got back to their bunks.

Jody wore jean shorts and a jean shirt with the sleeves rolled up. Not one goose bump graced her muscled arms. "OK, you city dwellers. Our first exercise is called Trust Your Neighbor." She winked. Jody talked as she walked, motioning for everyone to follow her. She stopped in front of a solid rock wall not far from camp.

"People, time to choose a partner. Here's the deal. One person hops into the harness, the other spots and holds the rope below. If the person on the wall slips and falls, the person below is responsible for guiding the climber until he regains his footing. Now watch me and Nash here."

Even though she was a big girl, Jody had no trouble adjusting the harness to fit herself as Nash readied himself to belay her rope so that she would be safe. As she began to climb, Jody shouted directions to the campers below. "If you're on the wall, swing back and try to find a foothold so you can continue climbing to the top."

Everyone was riveted as Jody pulled her way up the wall. At one point she demonstrated what happens when a climber loses footing.

"The climber starts to bump against the wall. However, with the help of your partner—in this case Nash, who is manipulating the ropes—you can find a place to put your foot."

Jody made it to the top quickly and gave an enthusiastic thumbs up to Nash.

Maeve was biting her nails the whole time. Her near accident in gym class was still fresh in her mind.

Avery tried to reassure her. "Look, Maeve. You can't really fall. The harness will protect you, and whoever is on the ground can pull the ropes to tighten everything."

Maeve breathed a big sigh of relief. She could see that Avery was right. The big challenge would be the climbing, but she wouldn't really be in danger at any time.

When Jody landed back on the ground she gave a few more safety instructions, warned against any horseplay on the wall or when being fastened into the harness below, and then announced, "I only ask two things from everyone. First, give it a try, and second, give it your best shot. You will be really surprised at what you can accomplish when you give it your all. And remember, you are not doing this alone. Your teammate on the ground is with you all the time, and Nash and I are here to help. Helmets are required. Now, who's first?"

Avery partnered with Katani and Billy T. with Sammy. Charlotte watched with interest, remembering that Avery and Billy had made a bet on who was fastest. Both Billy and Avery had rock climbed before so their friends were expecting an exciting race.

Avery looked at Billy as both stood at the bottom, waiting for the signal to climb. Billy was taller than Avery, but everyone knew that Avery was a speed demon.

At the signal, Avery flew up the wall. "Go, Avery, go Avery," the rest of the BSG chanted.

Charlotte couldn't even see where Avery was putting her hands and feet. But on closer inspection, she could see these little grips for your feet and hands to hold on to. Avery beat Billy to the top by a couple of seconds. Avery turned, "Say good-bye to your dessert, Billy."

Both swung back to the ground, but Billy wouldn't even look at Avery as she did a little victory dance. His face was still red, but not from the effort of climbing.

Nash joined them at the bottom. "Campers, were you racing?" he asked. Pause. "Well, yeah," Avery said hesitantly. "Is that against the rules? Nobody said anything," she said hurriedly.

Nash answered firmly, "We don't race on the wall at Lake Rescue, Avery. I can see that you and Billy have had training, but most of our climbers are inexperienced and racing is too dangerous for them. So concentrate on technique and keep safety first, people. No more racing," he admonished. Avery looked a bit sheepish and went to say something to Billy. But he had turned and walked away.

"I guess I can't win your dessert now, Charlotte," joked Nick.

"I don't bet on things I have never done before," Charlotte answered. "And this is my first time climbing for real."

"Well, good luck then." Nick flashed her a smile and began climbing.

Surprising herself, Charlotte made it up the wall fairly easily. She had never done anything like that before. Pushing aside her fear, she just inched up and up and up, not looking down, until she touched the top ledge where Nash knelt waiting for her. She slapped Nash's hand, then repelled back down to solid ground.

"Wasn't that fun?" Avery patted Charlotte on the back. "I wish we could do it again. What's next?"

"Sitting, and waiting until everyone else is finished," said Charlotte. She then settled onto a big rock, letting the sun warm her face.

When it was Chelsea Briggs' turn, no one was willing to

spot her. Charlotte felt just terrible for Chelsea, whose face was unreadable. When John, one of the other counselors, realized that none of the campers was going to offer to help Chelsea out, he quickly stepped in. Most of the kids probably thought that they wouldn't be able to belay someone her size. Charlotte knew there was no way she could help Chelsea out.

With John below guiding her, Chelsea climbed slowly and carefully. She was clearly strong. But lifting her own weight as she reached and grabbed for the grip, then pulled herself up, was turning out to be difficult.

After three missteps where she swung away from the wall, then back, trying to find another place to hold on, she called down. "I can't do it; I just can't." Charlotte could see that she was right on the verge of crying, but was doing everything in her power to hold it in. Katani, who had been watching Chelsea intently, felt for her classmate. Katani thought she would have died of embarrassment if that had been her.

Slowly, John lowered Chelsea to the bottom and helped her unhook her harness. Chelsea's cheeks were stained bright red. After pulling off her helmet, she went to lean on a big rock. Charlotte saw that her legs were shaking.

Maeve leaned into Charlotte. "That was awful. Chelsea must be so embarrassed."

"Good try, Chelsea," Isabel called to her. Isabel was the only one who dared approach Chelsea. "I almost gave up after falling once. I would have totally given up if Nick hadn't cheered me on."

Nick Montoya was helping everyone, and he really seemed to like doing it, thought Charlotte. Nick would make a great camp counselor—he almost looked like one because he was so tall.

When the Yurtmeister looked down and began freaking out at how high he was, Nick yelled up to him, "Hey! President Yurt ... gotta minute?"

The Yurtmeister broke out laughing and made it all the way to the top.

Nick caught Charlotte watching him. She was sure her cheeks turned bright pink, but Nick just gave her a wave and turned back to a girl he was coaching. He hadn't made her feel dorky at all.

"OK, fifteen-minute break," Jody called. "There's lemonade, water, and oranges under the tree. Got to keep your energy up."

"Energy up? Miss Drill Sergeant is going to kill us all off on the first day," Katani whispered to Isabel.

Charlotte chewed some orange slices, then sat on a flat rock where the BSG had all sprawled. "Did anyone bring sunscreen? I left mine in my bunk."

Maeve handed Charlotte a big tube of sun block. "Without it, I'd look like a big tomato by evening ... with about a thousand more freckles."

"Does anyone know what's next?" Avery tossed back the rest of her water.

"Who knows?" Katani grinned. "Just try not to embarrass Billy again, Avery. I think you might have hurt his feelings."

"Hey, he's the one who always wants to race, and I'm already up by one dessert," Avery defended herself. Then she ran to get a handful of the orange slices to take with them as Jody signaled the end of break.

"Isn't it great not to be sitting in school right now?" asked Avery as they all walked to the next activity. The BSG nodded in agreement.

"What?" Betsy Fitzgerald had heard Avery's comment.

"You don't miss school?" She looked at her watch. "We'd be in Ms. O'Reilly's class right now," she moaned. "But I suppose we are learning …"

"Wow, look at that." Maeve pointed. "I saw something like that on 'The Amazing Race,' although it was a lot higher and longer."

Between two platforms was a natural ravine. The idea was to grab hold of a trapeze bar, hold on for dear life, then slide to the lower platform.

"This is called the Flying Fox. I'm sure what you'll be doing here is obvious," Mia, the blond, peppy counselor explained. "Besides, it's not as hard as it looks, and falling off will be worse than holding tight and enjoying the ride," she joked. There really was no way that anyone could crash into the ravine because they were so securely fastened into a harness. Even if the harness broke, a second line would kick in. Still, it was a long way down.

"It does look like fun, doesn't it?" Charlotte got in line, close to the beginning.

"Speak for yourself," Chelsea murmured. She stationed herself next to the platform, ready to get some action shots. Suddenly, she decided the other side would be better, since she could see the faces of those coming toward her. So she hurried over the small bridge to the far platform, two camera cases dangling from her shoulder.

"She's going to take photos and hope no one notices she's not on the torture device," Isabel whispered.

"Good idea." Maeve grimaced. "I wish I'd have brought a camera."

As soon as Charlotte saw how much speed Billy Trentini picked up, she was ready to go ask Chelsea if she needed someone to hold her camera bag. She pushed Avery in front of her.

Avery waited until Nash placed a harness around her. If you slipped off the bar, the harness would catch you, but you'd have to be pulled slowly back to the top platform. Betsy had done that twice, then begged off, close to tears. She might get an E for effort, but no A for achievement on this activity.

Avery looked at Charlotte and grinned. "Watch this." She leaped off the platform, swinging her legs in front of her for momentum. To her surprise, she came way short of the far platform. What had happened? Was she too short to gain any speed?

Avery looked down, which had to be scary. She wasn't going to fall because of the harness, but the view was enough to make even "Her Braveness" swallow quickly a couple of times. Charlotte was breathing hard just watching. Billy Trentini stood at the far platform and looked on.

"Hang on, Avery. Hang on. Go back, try again. You can do it. I know you can." Well, that was a switch. The "competition thing" was gone. Billy was actually trying to help Avery.

After being pulled back on the other platform, Avery took a deep breath. She had to try again. Avery straightened her shoulders and took another leap. She swung her feet forward, but kept them still. This time she landed on the far ledge. She almost fell backwards, but Billy and John grabbed the bar to steady Avery and help her off just at the right moment. Billy raised his hand for a high five. Charlotte couldn't see Avery's face, but she slapped Billy's hand and slinked away.

From watching Avery, Charlotte knew this would not be easy. She got rigged up, grabbed the bar, and swung off the platform, not hesitating, not looking down. The wind swept her hair back. Her knuckles turned white. Her heart pounded as she picked up speed. Forcing her legs to stay ahead of her, she landed, leaned forward, and grabbed John's hand.

"Well done, Charlotte. Want to go again?" John asked.

She almost said yes. She had loved the rush of whizzing through the air, but people were waiting for their turns. "No thanks," she replied. "That was fun, but lots of people are waiting."

"Hey, Char," Avery half whispered. "Did you see how stupid I looked? I don't know what happened. That looked so easy."

Charlotte smiled. "It really was so much fun ... kind of like flying. Are you going to try it again?"

"Not today. It has to be time for lunch. And I'm on cooking duty." Avery took off at a jog.

"Mighty Mouse dethroned." Maeve walked up beside Charlotte. Katani and Isabel caught up. She and the other BSG had gone to the last cartoon fest at the Movie House, and they had all agreed that Mighty Mouse reminded them of Avery.

"That had to be embarrassing for her, but Avery can't be perfect at everything. Personally, I was sure they'd have to pull me up out of the ravine, in pieces. Did you see how many times I had to do that before I actually made it?" Maeve added dramatically.

"Yeah," said Isabel. "But you made it, Maeve of the Jungle."

"Good point," she answered as she high-fived Isabel.

"Hey look," Katani pointed to the Flying Fox. Betsy Fitzgerald was back for more. The girls could see the "no way will I be defeated" look in her face.

"I hope she makes it," said Isabel. "She will be really mad if she doesn't."

They watched as Betsy flew through the air ... and fell

just short of reaching the platform.

The girls could see Betsy's lip quiver. But a determined Betsy went back for more.

"Group finger cross," ordered Katani. Four set of hands hooked their little fingers together and crossed their fingers. "Go Betsy, go Betsy," they chanted.

A grinning Betsy gave them a thumbs up and went for it … across the ravine … would she make it … "Oh, yeah," shouted Maeve. John had to scoop Betsy up, but she made it.

The four girls gave her a major whoop.

"You have to admire that girl," Isabel proclaimed.

To the girls' dismay, there was yet another exercise before lunch. Jody was directing people to form a line as they came back to the fire circle.

"OK, the person in front of you is your partner," she informed them.

Chelsea had been expecting the worst, and it happened. She was paired off with Kiki, who glared at her as if Chelsea were dirt. Chelsea walked up, set down her cameras next to Kiki, and looked plaintively at Jody. But Jody had turned her attention to a couple of the boys who were fooling around. No such luck.

Couldn't the counselor see that a Chelsea/Kiki pairing was a disaster waiting to happen? Kiki Underwood was the snobbiest girl in the seventh grade. Even the Queens of Mean kept out of her way. Now here I am, Chelsea thought in a panic, paired with the one person most likely to make me feel really, really horrible.

Charlotte and Katani stood beside them. Charlotte could practically feel the sparks flying off Kiki.

"This is a trust exercise. Here's the plan. One of you is going to close your eyes and fall backward. Your partner is going to catch you. Obviously in order to fall back, you have to know your partner is going to catch you. Everybody ready?"

Kiki looked as if this was the most ridiculous thing she had ever been asked to do. She wanted to refuse. But about twelve kids were watching her. She pulled her bottom lip between her teeth, turned into a statue, and—before she could think about it—fell back into Chelsea's waiting arms. Chelsea had no trouble catching her. Kiki was a total lightweight in more ways than one, Isabel thought to herself. Chelsea pushed Kiki back to her feet, and Kiki jumped away immediately.

"OK, now switch partners, and repeat. Don't forget to relax."

Chelsea could see disaster coming a mile away. The Beacon Street Girls could too. But there was nothing anyone could do. How could they get Jody's attention without embarrassing Chelsea? Charlotte tried to wave to Jody but the counselor was helping some other kids.

"No way!" Kiki practically yelled. "No way will I even try to catch Chelsea … Chelsea Bigg … oops, sorry," she made a face. "I meant Chelsea Briggs. But, really. Is there anyone here who can catch her?"

Chelsea had had just about enough. "OK, Ms. Kiki Underpants, so I got a weight problem," Chelsea shouted angrily. "You don't have to be so rude about it."

Some kids started to laugh. No one had dared call Kiki "Ms. Underpants" since second grade. Anna and Joline laughed so loud, they began to snort. Clearly, Anna had never forgiven Kiki for trying to steal all the thunder in the talent show. Kiki was really mad. "You fat …"

Jody raced over and stepped between the two girls. "Enough, girls. This behavior is completely unacceptable. "We do not tolerate name-calling at this camp." She ordered

❀
139

✿

Kiki to partner with Tanya.

Charlotte, standing right next to Jody and Chelsea, overheard what Jody said next. "No one has to tolerate insults about the way they look. I know this is hard. But you don't have to let Kiki's comments bring you down. So let's go. Things are going to change for you ... I'm sure of it."

Chelsea closed her eyes, visibly relaxed, and fell back into Jody's arms. Chelsea couldn't stop a tiny smile from creeping onto her face.

Chelsea had just scored some major points with her classmates.

Later that morning, Josh Trentini told his brother, "It was a beautiful thing watching Chelsea take on Kiki 'Underfabulous' today."

"Yeah, but you better not let Jody hear you calling her Kiki Underfabulous—no name-calling remember," Billy reminded his brother.

Kiki was sitting on her bunk rebraiding her hair when Jody walked in. There was a certain look of defiance on Kiki's perfectly sculpted face.

But Jody had been there before. Rather than sit down on Kiki's bunk as she had planned for a heart-to-heart, Jody realized that this was a girl who needed the direct approach.

"Kiki, you seem like a smart girl so I am going to get straight to the point. It is against camp rules to taunt another camper—particularly about race, religion, or physical appearance. Are we clear about that? That is bullying, and it won't be tolerated."

Kiki turned her head and stared out the window.

"Kiki. I have sent campers home before for disobeying important camp rules. But, I think you can do better. Am I right?"

Kiki nodded. Her parents had gone to New York for vacation. They would be furious if they had to cut their trip short. Kiki picked up her mirror and checked her hair. Chelsea Briggs was so totally annoying, she fumed. But, whatever.

CHAPTER 12

☙

JODY AND CHELSEA'S INCREDIBLE SHRINKING ACT

"OK, ABOUT a half hour of free time until lunch," Jody announced. "Chelsea, help me make sandwiches, OK?"

"Sure." Chelsea was grateful she didn't have to help Kiki make sandwiches. How could Kiki be so incredibly mean? Chelsea began thinking that Kiki was under the spell of some wicked witch and that the only thing that would help was a good dunking in some ice-cold water. Hmm ... the lake. When could she get Kiki alone in a canoe? "Oh, oh," she could say. "I think Kiki fell out. I was so busy paddling, I never noticed. Has anyone seen her?" Chelsea smiled, reveling in the fantasy of Kiki taking a good dunking.

"I'm glad you can still smile at something," Jody said, passing Chelsea mayonnaise and a loaf of bread. Then Jody set out stacks of turkey, ham, cheese, lettuce, and sliced tomatoes, making an assembly line to be efficient. She opened up another loaf and quickly began to spread peanut butter and jelly on the slices.

Chelsea thought, I'm glad Jody can't hear what I'm thinking. She'd probably send me home. Actually, Chelsea would have loved to be sent home, except for the camera work she'd miss. Wait till everyone sees my pictures of the loons, she thought proudly.

"Just think twice before letting her win."

"Who?" Chelsea jumped out of her reverie.

"Whoever is bugging you." Jody grinned, as if she had no idea.

As they got the sandwich making under control, Chelsea decided to trust Jody just a little. "Remember what you said yesterday, Jody? That you were really fat when you were a kid?"

"Well, I said heavy. I don't use the word fat anymore. I think it's a mean thing to say, even to yourself." Jody reached in a back pocket and brought out a thin billfold. Carefully, after wiping her hand on her shorts, Jody pulled out a photograph and handed it to Chelsea.

Chelsea wiped her own hand, took the photo, and stared at it. There was no other word to use to describe the kid who was obviously Jody at about twelve. Jody was fat. Really fat. Chelsea, at her worst, was never so big.

Chelsea handed the photo back and Jody put it away. "What happened? You're in great shape. I mean, you're not skinny, but you look good. You know, healthy, fit. How did you ... and why do you carry that awful photo around all the time?"

"So I won't forget." Jody stacked finished sandwiches onto a platter. "I figured out I was never going to be a size 2, so I concentrated on being the absolute best, healthiest person I could be. My doctor told me that I was really at risk for diabetes (there was that word diabetes again, sighed Chelsea to herself). So, I figured that I would try and get healthy for awhile. I wouldn't worry about the 'the fat thing.' I would just respect my body and eat healthy and exercise. I decided that exercise would be the easiest to start with. So, I started hiking in the woods with my high school hiking group. At first, I was uncomfortable because I didn't know any of the kids and they were much better hikers than me. But it turned out that they were a really friendly group and everyone encouraged me. And, you know what? I loved it. I didn't just like it, I mean I really loved it. Loved being outside. Pumping up the hills. It was fun. Next, I gave up the soda. Stopped watching TV all day on Saturdays and Sundays. You know, that's when eating gets out of control for me. I watch TV, I eat. I eat, I watch TV. The two go hand in hand."

Jody could have been telling Chelsea's own story. She loved TV, and TV wasn't TV without a snack ... or maybe two or three.

"Anyway, I just kept getting healthier and happier and fitter and I realized what fun it would be to make a career out of the whole thing."

Chelsea nodded. "I like to walk ... When I miss my bus, I walk home from school. It gives me time to think."

"That's a great start. Maybe you could find a buddy to do that with. I used to have dance parties after school. A couple girls in my neighborhood who were also heavy came by. We had a ball."

"And remember, all snacks are not created equal. Someone told me if you don't get enough chewing, you don't feel satisfied, even right after a meal. That was so me, I didn't even try those liquid diets. Too boring. No fun at all. Instead, I made a list of crunchy snacks that took maximum chewing ... and that I liked. Like carrots. Love baby carrots—so much tastier than the grownup ones." Jody grinned.

"I like baby carrots too. I like to dip them in hummus."

Chelsea ripped open a new bag of bread. "How many of these sandwiches are we making anyway?"

"I figure most of the boys can eat two. They need to eat more to maintain their weight. Maybe we'll stop at fifty or sixty. We can always make more."

Chelsea knew she could eat two. Could she stop at one today? Or maybe, she would just try stopping when she had had enough. Maybe she would just slow down and see what happened. No pressure. That would make her want to eat more.

"Did you join any of those weight loss groups?"

"No, that wasn't for me. What I did join was a martial arts class. The idea of a license to kick some you-know-what appealed to me. In class, I could knock someone flat, and it was OK. I had to admit I was holding in a lot of anger and unhappiness. Strange to say, as I became happier, I wasn't as hungry. It's easy to eat when you're stressed or something happens that you feel you can't do anything about."

"Like someone calling you names or refusing to partner with you?"

"Exactly. I took a yoga class and I learned to meditate. Just sitting still without eating was a big accomplishment. Keeping your hands busy helps. Some people knit, but that wasn't for me."

"When I'm putting my pictures onto my computer and messing with them, I forget about eating."

"Exactly. Keep busy with something you really like to do."

"How long did it take you to lose as much weight as you wanted?"

"Two years, Chelsea."

"Two years?" yelped Chelsea.

"Listen, Chelsea. Take it from one who knows. You are

too young to even be considering a diet. Just eat some healthy food and get moving. It took me two years to change my life. It wasn't easy, and some days I fell back into my old ways. But I didn't stay there long and I knew that I wanted to feel better about myself. So I just kept going. Now, I just kind of eat healthy on a regular basis, stay away from too much junk, and keep active as much as I can. I'll never go back. That's why I look at that photo occasionally. Believe me, it sends chills down my spine to see that overweight, lonely kid—the kid that was me." Jody paused and looked sidelong at Chelsea. Then she asked, "Do you ever feel lonely?"

Chelsea didn't say anything for a long time. She could feel her pride keeping her from answering. But then she thought about how nice Jody was being to her and she figured maybe she would take a chance ... and trust someone just this once.

"Sometimes, I do. Mostly at school, I keep to myself there."

"You can feel terribly alone in a crowd. But, I'm not sure being lonely has anything at all to do with other people. I have a friend who just got married and moved away. She called me and said she'd never felt so lonely in her life."

"Maybe she married the wrong guy."

"No, he's a really nice man. She is shy and for the first time in her life she has to make an effort to get out there and meet new people. It's hard doing things you have never done before."

Chelsea thought Jody was one of the smartest people she had ever met. She seemed to know about how people really felt.

Jody looked over at Chelsea with a big grin. "You know, before I got healthy, I assumed boys only liked skinny girls."

"That's not true?" Chelsea looked incredulous.

"No it's not. Surprise! Guys like girls who are happy and confident and like to have fun." Then she laughed. "Most guys I know don't like to work too hard at relationships ... you know what I mean?" All of sudden Chelsea started to laugh. "What's so funny?" asked Jody.

"I was just thinking about my brother Ben and his girlfriend. Ben said he liked her because she made good pizza and she was the only girl who could catch one of his football passes." Jody howled at that one and Chelsea joined in. Lake Rescue just might be a turning point in my life, Chelsea thought as she began loading the sandwiches on the plates.

As she helped Jody carry the plates to the big table, Chelsea thought about how Nick Montoya looked at Charlotte. He liked her, you could tell that. But he wasn't real obvious about it. He just treated her as a friend. Who wouldn't like Charlotte, or any of the Beacon Street Girls for that matter? They were fun, laughing all the time, always thinking up something crazy to do. If Chelsea laughed more, would people like her? If she went to gym class and tried all the stuff, even if she looked stupid, would people say something like "Good try?" Unlikely, thought Chelsea wryly. Most seventh graders weren't that clued in.

"Have you got some particular boy in mind?" Jody interrupted Chelsea's thinking. She grinned at Chelsea.

"Oh, no. No boy—"

"Maybe not now. Try some of the other stuff first. The boys will come. If you give me your address, I know about an Outward Bound camp for kids. I went to one of their programs. That also helped to change my life. And after I got over being scared out of my mind by everything they were making us do, that camp was the most fun I'd ever had up to that point. That's a big reason I became a camp counselor here."

"Thanks for asking me to help make the sandwiches, Jody," Chelsea said, lifting another platter of sandwiches.

"If I give you my address or my email, will you write to me? I'd like to know how you're doing."

"Would you really write back?"

"Of course. And will you send me some photos from this week?" Jody asked.

"It's a deal."

Outside, Chelsea took a plate and a sandwich. She took a small handful of potato chips and piled on raw carrots, celery sticks, and an apple.

She found it hard to pass by the chocolate chip cookies, so this time she just took one instead of her usual three or four. Then she took a glass of iced tea instead of a cola drink. In a couple of hours, she would probably be starving, but she might as well give this healthy eating thing a try. For once it didn't feel like a punishment, and it seemed to have worked for Jody.

Nash made the announcements after lunch. "OK, listen up, green and blue teams. We are generously giving you one hour of free time. You can nap, write in those journals I know you brought with you, or just hang. Then report back here at two o'clock."

"Is that when we do basket weaving?" Henry Yurt asked.

"And how about making those little braided leather key chains?" Dillon remarked. "I promised everyone at home I'd bring them one."

"In your dreams," Nash said. "This is hard-core outdoor education."

"I told you this would be like having gym class for a week," Maeve said. "I could sleep all afternoon."

"I agree." Katani held her eyelids open. "Just this once, I choose nap time."

Maeve linked arms with Katani, and the two girls walked up the hill to their cabin. As they crawled into their bunks, their cabin mates trickled in behind them and flopped down to snooze or read for a while. Everyone was glad for the chance to rest. Just as Maeve's eyes were closing, the door burst open and slammed against the wall. Anna's and Joline's shrill voices pierced through the peacefulness.

"Ugh, it smells like feet in here!" Anna said loudly.

Joline giggled. "Yeah, it's not pretty."

"Then why don't you go take a nap outside," Katani replied, rolling over to get more comfortable.

Maeve burrowed into her sleeping bag with her headphones to drown out the Queens of Mean.

೧೪

After free time, Jody waved them together for yet another trust exercise … uugh. The BSG groaned.

"I trust all of you, you trust me," Isabel said. "I don't think we need to prove it."

"While you were sleeping we created this work of art," Mia explained, pointing to a huge spider-web wall of ropes. "Here's the plan. We're all on the same team. The goal is to get every team member to the other side. We're going to break up into threes for this exercise. Two of you take your third person and literally weave that person up and over the web, passing in and out of the ropes. I'm going to give you pieces of colored string so I can check that you've not taken any shortcuts."

"I saw this on TV," Avery said. "It's not easy. Better find two lightweight partners."

Chelsea was standing right behind Avery when she said that. Chelsea stepped away immediately.

Here we go again, thought Chelsea. And just a few

❀

minutes earlier, she had been feeling better than she'd felt in a long time.

"Jody, this is going to be good. But I left my best close-up camera in my bunk. I'm going to get it."

Jody, hands on her hips, looked long and hard at Chelsea. Then she shrugged. "OK, hurry back."

Chelsea wanted to run, but she walked as fast as she could. Instead of going inside her cabin, she walked behind it and leaned against the wall. She was just never going to win, was she? Tears began to well as she slid down to a sitting position. And suddenly she was so hungry that even a handful of baby carrots seemed like chocolate chip cookies.

"Chelsea?"

Chelsea hadn't realized that she wasn't the only one seeking refuge behind the cabin. "Katani?" Chelsea's eyes were blurry, but there was no mistaking the girl in shorts who, sitting like a grasshopper, seemed all arms and legs.

"What are you doing here?" Katani asked, as if it wasn't obvious.

"Avoiding the spider web," Chelsea dared her to say something.

"Sounds good to me."

"But *you* could do that rope, spider-web thing."

"Check it out, Chelsea. I'm all arms and legs. I'd be so tangled in a couple of minutes, it would take an army of people with giant scissors to get me out. So, I left … I didn't want to mess it up for the whole team."

Chelsea started to giggle at the picture Katani painted. "I wonder who dreamed up all these torture exercises."

Katani grinned. "It was probably a group effort. One mind couldn't possibly be so devilishly evil. But you would have gotten some great photos."

They sat quietly for a minute, then started giggling again.

"You really like taking pictures?" Katani asked out of the blue.

"I love it. I've started a picture-taking business in my neighborhood."

"Your own business?" Katani was impressed. "What's it like?" she asked.

"It's no big deal. I take pictures at kids' parties. I'm going to think of other possibilities."

"How about Bar or Bat Mitzvahs? Dog and cat photos? People are so goofy about their pets."

"Yeah, that's a good idea. I don't want this to get too big to handle, though. And I've really only just started."

"It won't if you plan your time right. I plan to have my own design business someday. I could help you if you need help with organization," Katani said shyly. "No charge. Or maybe we could trade. You could take some photos of us, you know, the Beacon Street Girls. And Marty. We have this crazy little dog that loves to do tricks. He kind of belongs to all of us."

Chelsea and Katani swapped ideas back and forth for a few minutes until they saw Mia walking toward them.

"Girls," she said, frowning, "you're not allowed to wander away from the group. There're a lot of you to keep track of. I know you two are responsible, but the rules are the same for everyone."

"Sorry, Mia," Chelsea responded.

"Yeah, we're sorry," Katani added.

Mia nodded and said, "Alright, let's head back to the group."

Suddenly, a thought occurred to Chelsea. For once, she'd made it through the rest of the afternoon without feeling as

✿

if she was going to starve to death. It was as if her connection to another person had just filled her up, and also made her appreciate who she was … a pretty cool person with a lot to offer. Chelsea smiled to herself. That was pretty amazing. Must be the New Hampshire mountain air, she reasoned.

CHAPTER 13

CR

THE CLOCK STRUCK TWELVE

NOBODY MENTIONED that Chelsea and Katani had missed the team spider-web weaving exercise, even though the Beacon Street Girls knew that Katani had disappeared. Katani was aware that they shouldn't have separated from the group, but she couldn't help but think that Chelsea seemed a lot happier after their talk.

"That was too cool, Katani." Avery grinned. "Billy just lifted me up and Charlotte held the ropes open for me to go in and out of. It was pretty easy."

"I was scared," Charlotte admitted. "First Dillon lifted Maeve, then he lifted me. Avery pulled the ropes apart, but I got dizzy before it was finished. At least we weren't racing." Charlotte looked at Avery and dared her to say she'd woven through the fastest.

"Nick helped me the entire way through," Isabel said. "I definitely trusted him not to drop me."

Charlotte had noticed that Nick seemed to be helping Isabel a lot lately. First on the wall and now this. She felt a twinge. Did Isabel like Nick? Charlotte would never let a boy come between her and another BSG, but she would be totally disappointed if Nick liked another girl. And if he and Isabel started going out, it would be even harder to take. After all, the BSG just assumed that eventually Nick and Charlotte would be an item even if it took them until twelfth grade.

But who knew if Nick really liked her, or if he was just the nicest boy ever? Although it wasn't as if Charlotte was chasing after him. And in front of everyone, Nick had made a big deal that he wanted to sit with Charlotte on the bus. So confusing. Charlotte rubbed her head.

She decided not to like Nick too much. Her life was finally in a smooth phase. Predictable. Comfortable. Like the stars were in the same place every night, or so close to the same place you could count on them being there. "Charlotte." Isabel elbowed her. "Aren't you hungry? I'm starving. Let's go see what's to eat."

"Wow, sloppy joes," Dillon announced as he got closer. "I feel like I haven't eaten in weeks."

"Can we get in line in front of him?" Maeve asked Jody, who was watching them inch up to be served.

"I think there's plenty. And the cooks only give out two at a time." Jody grinned.

"How come you're serving instead of eating?" Kiki whispered snidely to Chelsea. "You on a diet now?"

Chelsea glared at Kiki. She just couldn't believe the nerve of the girl. Everyone knew Jody had spoken to Kiki, and still she kept at it. Kiki seemed to be one of those people who never let up once they realized that they could needle you. Chelsea would just have to show Kiki how insignificant her comments were.

"Next in line, please. Hi there, you want one or two?" Chelsea politely asked the boy behind Kiki.

"Hey, you're holding up the line." The boy raised his voice to Kiki, who was staring at Chelsea. Kiki couldn't believe it. Chelsea Briggs, of all people, was ignoring *her*, and now some annoying boy was rushing her through the food line. How dare he!

"You're not the only one who wants something to eat you know," he said loudly to Kiki. His friends behind him began to chant, "We want food. We want food."

"Kiki, could you move along, please? We've got people to feed." Chelsea smiled ever so sweetly.

Jody was looking over at the holdup, so Kiki had no other alternative but to move or risk causing a bigger scene. There would be no sloppy joes for Kiki Underwood tonight. She went and made herself a turkey sandwich and sat down with Anna and Joline. "That Chelsea Briggs is really getting on my nerves."

"Why, Kiki?" Anna asked innocently.

Kiki looked at her sharply and took a big sip of milk. "Anna," Kiki said in her best sticky sweet voice. "You look like you've gained a few pounds up here."

"These sloppy joes are really good, Kiki," said Joline slyly. "You should try some."

"Whatever!" Kiki jumped up and went to sit at another table. She had a huge milk moustache, which sent Anna and Joline into gales of satisfied laughter.

Chelsea happily dished out sloppy joes until there were no more left. Then she grabbed a plate for herself, filled it with salad, turkey, and veggies, snatched a piece of bread, and walked over to where the BSG were sitting. She asked if she could join them. "Sure, no problem," said Katani. "Avery, move over and let Chelsea sit down." And they kept on talking like it was no big deal that Chelsea Briggs was sharing their table.

Shortly, Billy, Nick, and Dillon joined the table. Dillon looked a little sheepish as he stood across from Chelsea. Chelsea was feeling magnanimous so she decided to let him off the hook.

"Hey, Dillon," she said coolly.

"Hey Chels, how's it going?" he asked as he sat down next to Maeve, who beamed up at him.

"Pretty good," Chelsea answered.

It's going just great, Chelsea thought to herself. Just great. Standing up to Kiki had just about made her night. No fuss, no muss. No name-calling, a simple refusal to engage with the likes of Kiki Underwood. Yes, thought Chelsea. Things were just about perfect. Chelsea Briggs was on the move. She could just feel it.

"So what's going on for tonight?" asked Billy.

"Midnight hike, or something like that I think. Maybe we will hear the real ghost," Avery said with bravado.

"There's no ghost," Nick said as if he were correcting a group of foolish five-year-olds. "Whoever started that ghost tale probably didn't know about loons. And besides, loons are mostly noisy at dawn and at dusk." He finished his last bite of sloppy joe and then continued. "Sometimes they're claiming territory. The calls change if you listen really carefully."

"Whoa, Montoya," said the Yurtmeister, who had just joined them. "How do you know so much about loons, Mr. Looney Tunes?"

Crunching on a handful of corn chips, Nick responded, "I found a book in the camp library, Yurtster." Then he threw a corn chip at the class president's head.

"There's a library here?" Maeve asked. "I thought we

were supposed to get away from school."

"Well, it's really just a few bookcases in the counselors' lounge," Nick explained.

"Did you bring your laptop, Maeve?" Charlotte was curious.

"I did. I had to have a note from my mother, though, in order to bring it."

"Really?" Dillon said.

"I guess the camp counselors thought anyone with a computer would spend the entire time here writing emails back home to friends. But I get to write my journal on it ... you know ... the dyslexic gig," she shrugged.

"All your friends are here." Avery laughed. "Although ... You could write the brainiac."

"I already sent an email to Sam. They let me plug into the dial up at the office." Maeve shook her head. "As annoying as he is, he would be so bummed if I didn't write him. I told him about the haunting sound—he doesn't know about the loons yet. He's all excited that there might be a ghost here."

"I wish we could write to Marty," Avery said. She was almost serious.

"Send a postcard to a dog?" Billy Trentini said. "I can see it now. Dear Marty, wish you were here. There are lots of sticks and skunks to play with."

"If there are really skunks, don't let me near them. I didn't think I could top my last disaster, but walking into a skunk on a midnight hike would go to the top of the list." Charlotte hadn't done anything clumsy that could qualify as a calamity for some time now. That is, if you didn't count the time she dropped all of her books in front of Nick after the movie. She hoped she wasn't overdue for a catastrophe.

"OK, listen up, blues and greenies." Jody appeared at

their table. "The rumors are true. We really are going on a midnight hike. We could go right after dinner, but I think there's something magic about midnight. Head back to your bunks, catch some down time, and I'll sneak in and find you at the witching hour. Questions?"

"Do we—"

"Yes, you all have to go. This is part of the camp experience. You don't want to miss anything, do you?"

Katani, who had started to ask the question, rushed to correct the impression that she didn't want to go. "I really don't want to miss anything. But if I fall asleep, it's hard to wake me up. Midnight is late."

"There will be ice left in the drink tub. A refreshing wake-up call for Ms. Katani Summers, don't you think, men?"

Yurt addressed Dillon, Billy, and Nick when he said men. They looked like eight-year-old boys when they all grinned and nodded.

"You do not want to go there," Katani said, laughing. The idea of being awakened by a bucket of ice made her shiver.

The BSG all gathered in Charlotte's bunk for a visit. "It's almost like a sleepover in the Tower," said Maeve excitedly.

"You need to talk softer," said Tanya. "I want to read."

"Sorry, Tanya, we'll be more quiet," Charlotte assured her bunk mate.

The BSG chatted for awhile about the day's events until they all dozed off. When Jody came by at midnight it seemed like just a minute had gone by.

As Jody shook Charlotte's arm, Charlotte sat up quickly, knocked heads with Jody, and then fell back onto her pillow. "Oh, sorry, I'm so sorry."

"Hey, hardest part of my body. Time to get up, everybody. The forest awaits." Jody walked over and shook Chelsea, who had quickly put a pillow over her head.

"Five-minute pit stop, then gathering and counting heads at the campfire. No slackers," said Jody.

"That woman should have her own reality show." Maeve's voice sounded really tired as she stretched.

"Moonlight, darkness, Dillon." Charlotte said the magic words. Maeve grabbed her fleece coat, hugged it tight around her, and smiled to herself.

"I brought along some star charts for us to follow." Jody handed out cardboard wheels and paperback books. "But, you'll have to share."

"We really don't need star charts." Avery took one anyway. "We have Charlotte."

"We have a star master in our midst?" Jody asked. "Charlotte?"

"Not really. But my dad and I have always studied the sky wherever we lived."

"She's lived in Australia and Africa, and a bunch more places," Isabel said, falling in line with the group.

"And is a world class bragger," Kiki added when Jody was out of hearing range.

"Kiki," Maeve stood in front of her. "You need a serious attitude adjustment."

Kiki just flounced away. Nothing seemed to affect that girl.

"You want to be partners, Charlotte?" Chelsea asked, walking up beside Charlotte.

Charlotte hesitated for the slightest of seconds. She really wanted to be with one of the BSG, but she didn't want to be rude to Chelsea. So she said, "Sure, Chelsea. If you don't mind a ..." She hesitated for a brief moment and then said, "know-it-all."

"It's cool to know things." Chelsea dropped back so they were nowhere near Kiki. "And Kiki is just probably jealous because you've traveled so many places."

"Maybe Kiki is mean to you because you are so good at photography." Chelsea wondered if that could possibly be true.

"My goal is to go to every continent before I'm twenty-five!" added Charlotte. "Have you ever been out of the United States, Chelsea?" Charlotte asked.

"No. My mother keeps talking about going somewhere once she sells a couple more houses. She's a real estate agent. Her latest idea was one of those health spas."

"Where they soak you in mud and then wrap you in seaweed? Sounds ..." Charlotte scrunched up her face.

"That's what I thought. Plus they starve you to death. I'd rather go on a cruise."

Chelsea found herself giggling with a classmate for the second time in a day. Over a day, remembering that it was now past midnight.

"Look, Chelsea." Charlotte stopped them a short distance behind Jody and the rest of the hikers. "I've never seen so many stars in the city without a telescope. There's my favorite. Orion. See those three stars? That's his belt. As the story goes, he's up there because Apollo didn't like him and tricked the goddess Artemis into killing him. She loved him and was broken-hearted, so she placed Orion in the sky as a constellation."

"Kind of like the Cree warrior trying to get into heaven," Chelsea added, "but no one helped him."

As if on cue, the tremolo voice of the loon floated into the clearing where they stood stargazing. This time, the loon sent a little magic into the mix of silence, stars, and the smell of spruce and fir trees. The group hushed, hardly breathing.

After a reverent pause, John took over talking and pointing to the sky. Charlotte and Chelsea moved up to listen to the star lecture.

Charlotte wanted to freeze the moment—to place it into her best of all experiences.

As they headed back to camp, Nick took Charlotte's arm and stopped her. He pointed upward. "Isn't that another of your favorites?"

How did Nick know she liked the Seven Sisters almost as much as Orion? She didn't remember telling him.

A solitary cloud drifted by, like a curtain pulling aside to reveal the beginning of a long-anticipated Broadway show. The constellation of the Seven Sisters marched across the sky.

"I read that Zeus changed the sisters into stars to help them escape the attention of Orion."

"You think that helped?" Charlotte asked.

"No, not if he really cared for one of them and not if he really wanted to find her."

She didn't ask how Nick knew she liked "the sisters." She didn't speak. That would have spoiled the moment. And she didn't protest when he took her hand and followed the campers, now noisy and laughing ahead of them.

Like Castor and Pollux, the twin stars, Charlotte and Nick formed their own little constellation as they walked slowly along the path toward the camp.

CHAPTER 14

LOONS, MOOSE, AND SWEET REVENGE

EARLY the next morning, Charlotte was awakened to a "Pssst, pssst," outside her cabin. What time was it? Early. Too early. It seemed like they had just gone to bed.

"What? Who is it?" She slid out of her sleeping bag and bunk and staggered to the door. The hinges creaked something awful. The counselors probably left them rusty so they could hear people escaping.

Nick's grinning face greeted her. "Get up and get dressed. We're going to see the loons. You don't want to miss seeing them."

Yes she did. Right now, at least. "Give me five minutes."

"OK, but hurry. And see if Isabel wants to come."

Charlotte bit her lip. Nick's inclusion of Isabel immediately took away the magic. But as soon as she had that thought, she pushed it aside. She felt selfish. Of course, Isabel should go.

"Isabel, Isabel, wake up. Shhhh. Get dressed fast. We're going to see the loons."

Isabel sat up, rubbed her eyes, then came to life. "Oh, I've been dying to see them. Who—"

"Nick is outside the cabin. Hurry up!"

As it turned out, a whole group of seventh graders were waiting outside in the early morning light and fine mist, which gave Charlotte shivers but seemed perfect for their trip. Could this be their odyssey? No, there was no hardship involved, she thought, and the loons had already been discovered.

Just as that thought raced through her mind, one called. Oooo, ooo, oooo, ooo, oooo, ooo.

Was there a stranger sound in nature? Maeve looked over at Charlotte, scrunched her shoulders, and grinned.

Near the lake, the group hunched down and flattened themselves in the grass. They were going to get wet, but thank goodness, not muddy.

Oooo, ooo, oooo, ooo, oooo, ooo.

The call came from a different direction.

"That's another loon calling back. They talk to each other," Nick whispered.

Avery quickly turned around. "Spooky, just too spooky." She ducked the fake punch coming from Billy Trentini.

"Think we can get closer?" Dillon asked.

"I don't think so. They probably know we're here. And I read that they are very shy. But maybe they're used to people from the camp." Nick slid forward about a foot. "We can try."

Charlotte took the binoculars that Dillon passed her. As

she focused, the black and white bird with the checkered back leapt close, making her catch her breath at its beauty. His head was black, his eye red, and he wore a collar of black and white.

Nick whispered. "He'll lose the checkered back in winter. Then he'll be mostly black. Of course, he'll fly south soon."

Billy inched too close. Both birds rose with a flapping of wings and a splash of the lake water.

"Ahhh!" Billy yelped as something moved in front of him. "What? Geesh, Chels, I thought you were a—a rock—a gray rock."

Chelsea, clad all in gray sweatpants, a gray sweatshirt, and a gray rain slicker, stood up. "Scared yah?" She buckled her camera into its case.

Even in the dim light, Charlotte could see Billy's face turn red. "Well, not really. I was just surprised, you know. It's dark out here still."

To everyone's relief, Chelsea laughed. "Is everyone out here? Good thing I got here before you spooked them."

"Sorry 'bout that," Billy said. "Did you get some good photos? Does that camera take close-ups?"

"It has a zoom and I got some really good shots. Want to see them?" Chelsea turned on her camera and backed up the photos until she got to where she had started photographing the loons.

Everyone gathered round and looked at them. "Wow, Chelsea," Charlotte said. "Those are awesome. How can I get one?"

"I can email them to any of you once I get home and put them on my computer. Just give me your addresses."

"That's really cool," Nick said. "We better get back; it's getting late. We'd better get back before we get caught."

They didn't get caught, but they did get ratted out at breakfast.

"They sneaked out early this morning, Jody. I watched them. I didn't go, of course," Kiki announced.

"Did they invite you?" Jody surprised Kiki with her question.

"Well, no, but I never would have gone." Kiki quickly turned and walked away.

"Chelsea, you went on this field trip?" Jody said 'field trip' with a question in her voice about this early excursion being all about appreciating nature.

"Yes. I was taking photos." Chelsea looked at the BSG, minus Katani, and smiled. "We all just wanted to see the loons up close. They are so beautiful and Nick read up about them." Chelsea was going on and on like she was trying to keep everyone from getting in trouble.

"No more early morning trips without a counselor … got that, campers?" Jody's hands gripped her hips.

"I swear on … on … on," Chelsea couldn't think of anything and then it just popped out, "my mother's real estate license." The corners of Jody's mouth twitched, but she kept a straight face.

Chelsea couldn't believe she had said such a dumb thing.

"OK, breakfast, and you'd better have some good pictures to email me when you get home."

"She does, Jody," Billy Trentini said. "She has some awesome ones. I'll bet she could sell them to some nature magazine."

Chelsea's cheeks flushed with pleasure at Billy's compliment.

"I wish I had come with you guys," Katani said. "I just couldn't get out of bed. Chelsea, you really *should* sell your pictures. You could make some good money."

Chelsea looked at her funny.

Katani looked suddenly embarrassed. "I know I must sound like a nerd, but I really want to start my own business someday. I could help you if you want."

This was the second time Katani had offered to help her. Maybe, thought Chelsea, I'll take her up on it when we get back. You never know, she figured, I might really sell my photos someplace really cool. Chelsea walked quickly to the dining hall. She wanted to get photos of kids eating ... and making faces. Everyone loved those kinds of goofy pictures.

Katani invited Chelsea to sit with the BSG at breakfast after she finished shooting.

"Katani will put us all to work before we're fifteen," Isabel said. "She keeps telling me I could sell my crafts. And I keep telling her that I'd rather spend my time making more crafts instead of worrying about selling them."

"Well, it's good that we're all different. It'd be pretty boring if we were all clones who liked the exact same things!" Charlotte remarked.

When breakfast was over and the dishes had been washed, Jody blew her whistle and gathered teams together. "Campers, we're going canoeing."

"On the water?" Betsy asked.

Everyone stared at Betsy for a few seconds. Jody was the first to recover. "Yes, we'll take the canoes to the lake for this experience, Betsy."

Avery rolled her eyes at the other BSG and grinned. "Where are they stored? Let's go right now. I love canoeing."

The canoe parade looked like five aluminum caterpillars with six legs each. Even funnier was that they were all wearing orange life preservers ... caterpillars with life preservers. Nick peeked out from the lead canoe to follow Jody, Nash, and John. Mia went off to help another group with more trust exercises.

The fog had lifted and the sun came out on one of the most beautiful Indian summer days that any of the kids could remember. A few trees had colored leaves holding tight, while the ground around the lake was a patchwork of fallen leaves.

Chelsea photographed people dividing up and taking off. Then she stowed her camera in her bag and left it under some bushes beside the shoreline. A pile of coats and excess gear also awaited their return.

John led the regatta, telling them if they eased through a narrow passageway, they'd come out on a much bigger lake. And if they stayed quiet and let only the swish of paddles fill the air, they might see other birds or animals along the shore.

Once Charlotte, Nick, and Isabel learned to work together and get a rhythm going with their paddling, they skimmed the water silently and were the first to enter the narrow waterway that John pointed out.

At times, they actually pushed against the shore to slide through, but gliding out into the larger lake made Isabel gasp.

"Look," Isabel whispered. "There's a moose. A real moose!"

Sure enough, near the bank to their left, an enormous moose with a huge rack of paddle-like horns stood ankle deep, if moose have ankles, in the water and grazed on plants. He grabbed a mouthful, lifted his head, water streaming from the greens, and looked at the campers.

"Don't even think of getting close," Nick whispered. "John told me they're very dangerous. But if we don't threaten him—"

✿

"We get the idea," Charlotte said. "Don't moose around with the wildlife." It was a terrible pun, and she and Isabel giggled, while Nick shook his head. "Bad. Very bad."

Everyone knew to give the moose a wide berth, and soon they were past him on the other side of the lake. As all the canoes caught up, Charlotte noticed that Chelsea had ended up in a canoe with Kiki and Joline. It was like Chelsea was doomed to walk under the black cloud of Kiki Underwood forever.

All of a sudden Chelsea accidentally dropped her paddle. "Oh, darn," she said, reaching into the water for it. "I'll get it." Her foot on the side of the canoe and Chelsea's shifting weight was all it took to tip the balance. Over they all went. Chelsea came up laughing, and didn't care one bit that she was soaking wet.

But Kiki. That was another story. There was a whole lot of screaming going on.

"You fat idiot, Chelsea. You did that on purpose. I know you did. I saw you."

"Be quiet," yelled Joline. "We'll both get kicked out of camp if you keep insulting her."

Chelsea swam over to the canoe, hefted it upright, balanced on the edge, and swung herself over into the shell. The move was as graceful as any Charlotte had ever seen her make. What made Chelsea think she couldn't do anything in gym class? It took skill to right a canoe and get back into it.

"Want a hand?" Chelsea offered to pull either Kiki or Joline into the boat. Clearly the answer was no.

Both wet campers ignored her and floundered onto shore, which wasn't so far away.

"What happened, Chelsea?" Jody tied up her canoe to a buoy near the shore and waded in to check on Kiki and Joline.

"I ... I ... it all happened so fast. I dropped my paddle and it started to drift away. When I reached out to grab it, I guess I tipped the canoe. Then we all fell out."

"Did anyone else see the accident?" Nash questioned the kids nearby.

No one really had. Anna sat, wide-eyed, staring at her two very wet friends, whose hair was a mass of tangles. She could hardly contain her pleasure at the sight of Kiki sopping wet and mad ... so mad. It just about made Anna's day, especially since Kiki was always trying to butt her way into her friendship with Joline.

"Well, no harm done, I guess," Jody said. "There are a few towels in the plastic bag in my canoe. Someone get out a couple for Kiki and Joline. It's good thing it's so warm today."

Nick jumped into Jody's canoe and got the towels. He threw one to Chelsea. "You OK, Chelsea? You didn't have your camera, did you?"

Chelsea put the towel around her hair turban style, squeezed, then toweled off her arms and legs. "No, I left it where we started off. I'm OK. It's getting warm. I'll dry off."

"I really messed up, huh," Chelsea confided sheepishly to Charlotte, who had paddled to the shore.

"I know how you feel," Charlotte said. "I'm always so embarrassed when other people pay for my disasters."

Chelsea hoped Charlotte didn't think Chelsea had tipped the boat on purpose. Chelsea thought Kiki had been beyond mean to her on this trip. And honestly, how much could one person take? But Chelsea didn't want anyone to think that she was the kind of person that used revenge to get even. She was better than that. And, she would never risk someone drowning.

"I wish the water was warm enough for all of us to

swim," Avery said, paddling her canoe closer to Chelsea and Charlotte. "But when I put my hand in, out there where it's deep, it's pretty cold. I guess I'll just stick my feet in."

Jody, Nash, and John gathered the canoes into three smaller groups. After trying to coax them back into a boat, the counselors let Kiki and Joline sit on the grass to dry off. Chelsea decided to stick it out, especially to prove she was tougher than Kiki and Joline. Some of the groups studied the plant life around the lake's edge. Some hiked a little way into the woods, exploring. Nash organized canoe racing, the most popular activity, especially with Avery and the Trentini brothers. Because they had brought lunches, every group took part in every activity. There was even time for a short nap after lunch.

The day was lazy and much less threatening than the one before. No one had to trust anyone. The competition was not serious, and everyone had a notebook full of leaves, flowers, sketches, and journal entries. Isabel showed some of the girls how to press flowers tightly between the pages of their notebooks so they would dry and stay pretty for a long time. Nick Montoya suffered through some serious teasing just so he could bring a pressed flower back to his mother.

When they returned to camp, Jody announced free time until dinner. Tired and a little baked from the warm autumn sun, the BSG made their way slowly to their bunks. Avery was the only one who acknowledged the big event of the day.

"Funny show, Chelsea." Avery held up her hand and Chelsea slapped a high five.

"Anytime, Avery," Chelsea said, "... anytime."

I can't believe I dumped Kiki and Joline in the water. It really was an accident. I never would have done something like that on purpose. But, honestly, I'm not really sorry. Nobody was hurt and every time I think of the water and goo streaming down Kiki's face, it just makes me laugh out loud. That Kiki—what a cold fish ... hahaha!

Kiki has so much experience being mean, but at least she's honest. Everyone knows where they stand with her, which is nowhere. I'll get there someday. Not mean like her. You know, just being able to be honest.

And this morning. I didn't even mind Billy thinking I was a rock. Plus, he was truly embarrassed. I was lying so still, I probably did look like a gray rock in the mist. Besides, Billy liked my photography. I wonder if I really could be a wildlife photographer. I loved watching those loons and getting photos of them. Animals don't give you the hard time people do, and I could get outside and hike to find them, like Jody suggested I do.

Jody is really cool. She has given me lots of things to think about. I know I eat when I'm feeling bad, but I didn't know how to stop doing that. Now I have a few ideas.

I thought I'd be totally miserable at Lake Rescue, but I'm actually having fun. And it's true. When I feel good, I'm not hungry. Well, I mean I'm hungry, but I don't feel like I have to eat chips all the time. I can't explain it. It's just different. That must be the whole emotional eating thing Jody was talking about. Wow, I could write a book here with what I've learned. I would call it "Meditations from a Fat Girl."

No—wait a minute. What did Jody say? No calling yourself that. I'll just call it "Meditations from Chelsea" and I'll make it all pictures and have some cool quotes.

It's not New Year's, but who says I can't make some resolutions? Start my own new year. I might not keep all of them, but writing them down can remind me to try.

1. *Ask Mom to buy me some healthier snacks.*
2. *Save my money to get a better camera.*
3. *Walk and bike to school as much as I can.*
4. *Ask Mom if I can join a health club where they have weights. I want to be strong like Jody so I can climb the wall.*
5. *Write to Jody. I'm sure she meant it when she said it was okay, and that she'd write back.*
6. *Ask Mom if I can go to some sort of Outward Bound camp next summer.*
7. *Accept that I weigh about a thousand pounds and that someday I won't.*
8. *And maybe I'll even talk to my doctor about the whole "weight management" thing. I'm sorry, but that is such a weird thing to call it. Why do adults have to make everything sound so official?*

Chelsea went to bed with a smile on her face. She knew she'd have to take her resolutions one step at a time, but that it would be worth it. She finished her journal entry by listing all the good things that had happened since she got to camp. She started with Kiki Underwood falling in the water.

CHAPTER 15

છ

ADVENTURE AND MISFORTUNE

BY THURSDAY morning, the BSG were getting into a total camp-style rhythm. They had treated themselves to showers the night before and woke feeling like they could face anything the day brought. Alright, almost anything.

After breakfast Jody made announcements. "Campers, listen up. Today is your final big adventure. Everybody, get into your teams. Blue team. You are going to climb the mountain with John and Mia as your leaders. John is an experienced mountain climber, and Mia has done a lot of hiking in the White Mountains. Of course, this isn't serious technical climbing. But, it will be an all-day hike."

Charlotte felt a surge of excitement fill her stomach and stir up her bacon and eggs every which way. She loved climbing on mountain trails. She loved setting that goal of reaching the top and then achieving it. "And the green team ... is going swimming and sunbathing?" Henry Yurt suggested.

"In your dreams." Jody paused for some suspense. "The green team is going on an all-day hike to a swampy area which is farther away than the top of the mountain, but the terrain is mostly flat. And the bird life there is exceptional."

"Which group are you going with, Jody?" Chelsea asked.

Jody paused for effect. "I've earned a day off to go swimming and sunbathing. Actually, I have some reports to catch up on today. Your leader for the hike will be your science teacher, Ms. Weston, who is a birder, and Nash, who is an experienced wilderness hiker."

"Ms. Weston!" A few kids exclaimed. No one had even seen their science teacher since they had arrived.

"You probably wondered where she'd gone off to," continued Jody. The BSG looked at each other and all of them had to stifle a giggle. The fact of the matter was that they had been so busy they had completely forgotten about Ms. Weston. Charlotte felt a little guilty. She imagined that no one would like to be forgotten.

"Ms. Weston," Jody announced proudly, "has been working with the New Hampshire forest rangers and is eager to share what she has learned with the green team. I'm sure it's going to be an exciting time." Jody walked off to give directions to the other teams.

"I'll bet," Dillon whispered. "Isn't this the very same student teacher who got us lost going to the auditorium to see a film last week?"

Everyone around Dillon, including Maeve, giggled. "Maybe she is better at directions when she can see the sun or the stars."

"I wish I was going with the green team," Isabel said as they gathered their backpacks. "I don't know if I can climb a whole mountain in a day."

Nick reached out and punched Isabel gently. "Sure you can, Izzy. And if you get stuck, I'll help you."

Charlotte found yet another feeling churning inside her

already overloaded nervous system. *Izzy?* Charlotte mused. Was a small green monster growing larger inside her?

"So will I, Isabel," Charlotte added. "I've hiked a lot with my father. We've climbed a lot of mountains. The rule is one step at a time, sometimes resting between each step."

Nick grinned at Charlotte. "That's for something like Mt. Kenya or Kilimanjaro, isn't it?"

Charlotte flushed. Had she sounded like a know-it-all again?

Even though they were excited about the hike and mountain climb, the BSG were not thrilled about being separated for an entire day.

"Remember that part of going on an odyssey is misfortune." Maeve screwed up her face to suggest tragedy, but exaggerated the emotion so much that she had everyone around her laughing.

"Aren't you being a little bit over the top?" Joline said. "How can you guys be attached at the hip all the time? It's so juvenile."

"That's calling the kettle black," Avery said. "You and Anna are never apart. But anyway, I wish I was climbing the mountain, too. Walking to some swamp isn't much of a challenge."

"It could be. You could see a red-bellied woodpecker," Dillon teased.

"Or a duck-billed dinosaur who has been freshly cloned and reintroduced to Lake Rescue." The Yurtmeister opened his mouth to name other possibilities, but Ms. Weston cut him off.

"All right, greenies. How many of you have binoculars?"

Charlotte handed her binoculars to Katani. "Here, you can use mine. Not only will that lighten my pack, but looking at rocks close up isn't as much fun as birds or squirrels, or for that matter, dinosaurs."

"We might see the swamp ghost," Billy Trentini suggested.

"How about the Creature from the Black Lagoon?" Maeve started listing swamp monster movies as they prepared to leave.

John got their attention. "Each of you is responsible for your own backpack. Don't forget water, an extra layer of clothing, a whistle, a compass if you have one. Ms. Weston has the lunch pack for the greenies, and I have the lunch pack for the blue team. But you should grab some high energy snacks from the canteen."

"Like chocolate?" Charlotte asked hopefully.

"Only if it's wrapped around a protein bar or has some nuts. Chocolate kicks up your blood sugar, but drops you down twice as hard. Anyone have gorp?"

"Is that a fish or leftover barf?" asked Dillon.

"Gorp is a mix of peanuts, raisins, or other dried fruit, and M&Ms. There's your chocolate, Charlotte. I have a few extra bags." John handed them around. "Please share."

"Billy, why don't you grab the lunch pack and we will all take turns carrying it on the trip," Ms. Weston requested.

Suddenly Jody clapped her hands for everyone's attention.

"Campers … I must have your attention now. Before we all leave on this hike, the rangers have given us each a copy of the hiker code of responsibility. I am going to read it out loud and it's very important that you all follow it. Every year the state spends thousands of dollars and asks rangers to risk their lives to save lost hikers. So listen up!"

Hiker Responsibility Code

1. **With knowledge and gear.**
   Become self-reliant by learning about the terrain, conditions, local weather, and your equipment before you start.

2. **To leave your plans.**
   Tell someone where you are going, the trails you are hiking, when you will return, and your emergency plans.

3. **To stay together.**
   When you start as a group, hike as a group, end as a group. Pace your hike to the slowest person.

4. **To turn back.**
   Weather changes quickly in the mountains. Fatigue and unexpected conditions can also affect your hike. Know your limitations and when to postpone your hike. The mountains will be there another day.

5. **For emergencies.**
   Even if you are headed out for just an hour, an injury, severe weather, or a wrong turn could become life threatening. Don't assume you will be rescued; know how to rescue yourself.

6. **To share the hiker code with others.**

www.hikesafe.com

There was another mock-tearful good-bye for the BSG. Complete with mopey faces.

"Good grief," Anna said. "Joline and I have to split up for the day and you don't see us carrying on like that."

"Joline is probably relieved," Katani whispered to Chelsea.

Chelsea was impressed that Katani let Anna's comment roll off her back. She'd have to learn that little trick herself. Life would be much easier, she thought, if you could ignore the people who were annoying. Of course it was much easier to ignore an insult if you had a group of friends around who were supporting you. *All in good time.* Chelsea was suddenly reminded of her grandmother's favorite phrase.

As they trailed behind the green group, Chelsea showed Katani two digital photos of the group's gathering. "I have two extra discs, and an extra battery, but this camera holds sixty-four photos. A good photographer is supposed to take tons more photos than she uses. The nice thing about going digital is that you don't have to print the bad pictures."

"The ones of someone's backside?" Katani laughed. "We better hurry up. Remember the code—no separating from the group." Her long legs began to set a strong hiking pace and Chelsea struggled to keep up.

Chelsea was relieved not to have to climb a mountain, glad not to be climbing a wall or weaving through ropes, and determined to have a good time. She vowed not to eat her whole bag of gorp at once. She would parcel her gorp out in small handfuls to keep her energy up. Those M&Ms sure were tempting, though.

For awhile there was a whole lot of punching and pushing, laughing, and shoving going on. Maeve stopped to add a new dance step to the mix.

"My new hiking boots feel great. They're really

comfortable since I wore them around before we left to break them in. I'm glad Mr. Ramsey made me be sensible for once and get these instead of the pink ones. And he found me these hot pink shoelaces."

"I wondered if some shoe manufacturer was color-blind." Dillon laughed, but occasionally he'd stop and break into a dance routine with Maeve.

"Please stay focused, group, and quiet." Ms. Weston frowned at Dillon and Maeve. "I have heard about a sighting of a ruby-crowned kinglet still here in this area. Usually they've moved farther south by now. What a red-letter day it would be to see one. They are fairly hard to find. In any event, I've never found one."

"What does a ruby-crowned kinglet look like, Ms. Weston?" Billy Trentini kept a remarkably straight face when he asked. "Is it anything like a loon?"

"Oh my, no. While it inhabits swampy areas, it's not a waterfowl. It's a perching bird. If I see one, it will go on my birder's life list."

No one, not even the Yurtmeister, could think of a funny comment about "life lists." While birding wasn't on Chelsea's life list of things she wanted to do, she understood being passionate about something. Her love of photography was growing every day. Not only had Katani helped her see some ways of expanding her vision, but Jody had said it's good to have something you love to do. "It fills you up," she had said.

"Where are you going, Ms. Weston, if you don't mind my asking?" Nash asked.

Chelsea snapped a photo of the pretty young teacher staring through her binoculars as she eased off the path and into the woods.

"Shhh, do you hear that song?" Ms. Weston spoke

without taking her focus off the trees ahead of her.

"They're playing my song," Dillon whispered.

Maeve giggled and that set off Katani. Soon the entire green team was laughing softly.

"What does it sound like?" Avery asked.

Anyone could see that Avery was about to explode. She could have run to their destination and back by now. She wore off a little energy by sparring and racing back and forth with Billy, but Ms. Weston had cautioned them about getting split off from the group. As if they could. A blind rat in a complex maze could have found the green team at the snail's pace they now were moving at.

Ms. Weston had no idea people were teasing her. "It's kind of a husky ji-dit, ji-dit. The song is quite loud. Three or four high notes, several low notes, and then a chant. Tee, tee, tee, tew, tew, tew, tew, ti-dadee, ti-dadee, tidadee."

Yurt nodded. "OK." He cupped his hand around one ear and listened intently. "Is it a soft ti-dadee or a shrill ti-dadee?"

"Oh, it's very musical." Ms. Weston turned and walked back to the group.

"We better keep walking, Natalie. We've got to reach our marker within the hour."

"Yes, of course, Nash. It's so hard to keep a birder on track once they are on the hunt of a rare specimen."

The entire team was about to erupt into laughter, but they didn't dare. If Ms. Weston had indeed found her "life bird," they really didn't want to spoil it for her. Obediently they followed the counselors down through the woods, through a small swampy meadow where they had to watch their footing, and into the woods on the other side. Then they waded through some tall, wide-bladed grass and skirted an alder and maple swamp.

Beyond the water, they entered a thicker stand of evergreens, beeches, and oak. The leaves underfoot didn't give them away to the elusive bird, since they were wet and matted down from the earlier mist and fog. Occasionally, an outcropping of granite gave them a place to rest for a few minutes and watch Ms. Weston searching for her bird.

BLUE TEAM KLUTZ ATTACK

John looked at the kids surrounding him and shouted at the top of his lungs, "Is the blue team ready?"

Isabel, startled, jumped up from loading her backpack and let out a little yelp.

Josh Trentini screamed back even louder than John, "We're ready!"

Joline stuck her hand on her hip and rolled her eyes. "This is going to be painful ... extremely painful. Can we *please* get going so we can get it over with?" She slung her backpack over one shoulder and started walking toward the foot of the mountain. She hoped Anna was working as hard as she was.

"Hold on a minute, Joline," John said. "We have to make sure we're not missing anything important." He read out a list of the blue team's names to make sure everyone was there, and then packed the group's lunch in his backpack. "Now, does anyone have to go to the bathroom? From now on, it's just you and the great outdoors, so I'd suggest you all take the 'trip.'"

Charlotte, Isabel, and Betsy hurried to their cabins, while the boys jogged off in the opposite direction. Joline sat on a rock, looking annoyed, and pulled a fashion magazine out of her backpack.

When they all gathered together again, they set off,

walking up through the trees to the base of the mountain.

"Remember to watch out for poison ivy," John warned the group as they trekked up the steep path. He pointed to the three-leafed plant. "No one will want to dance with you tonight if you're itching like crazy. Even though it's not contagious."

Nick leaned over to Charlotte, who was walking with her head down to keep a close eye on the rocks and sticks lying precariously in the path.

"Hey Char ... would you dance with me if I had poison ivy?" he whispered.

Charlotte tried to will her face from turning red, but she had no such luck. "Maybe," she whispered back.

As she turned to smile at Nick, her foot caught on a tree root, and she tumbled forward. Out of the corner of her eye, she saw Nick lunge forward to try to catch her, but it was a pure Charlotte moment.

"Hey Char, you alright?" Isabel dropped down on her knees to put her hand on Charlotte's shoulder.

Charlotte buried her head in the dirt for a minute. "I'm fine," she replied. Isabel and Nick took her arm from either side and helped her up.

Charlotte turned to Isabel as she brushed dirt off herself and realized that Isabel had covered her mouth with her hand.

"Are you laughing at me?!" Charlotte exclaimed.

"I'm sorry," Isabel said, her voice shaking with laughter. "It wouldn't have been funny if you had been hurt. But you ... you looked so hilarious!"

Charlotte had to giggle. She was a little embarrassed, but she knew that it was probably better to laugh than be angry or upset. And it *was* pretty funny.

"I better walk a little closer to you from now on," Nick said. "I almost caught you before you took a dive. Sorry ... I mean, before you ... had your little accident."

Charlotte grinned and punched Nick lightly on the arm. Despite the rough start, she could tell that it was going to be a fun day.

GREEN TEAM FINDS THE RUBY

Suddenly, Nash halted the group. His brow was furrowed and he seemed to be a bit ... confused. Resting his pack on a log, he unzipped the front compartment and pulled out a map. Ms. Weston rushed over. "What's the matter, Nash? Are we lost? I thought we followed the correct trail."

"We did," he answered. "But we should be here," he said, pointing to a marker on the map for a trail head, "and we are not. There is something very wrong."

"I ... are we really off the trail? Do you know where we are, Ms. Weston?" Avery asked with concern in her voice.

Ms. Weston took the binoculars from her eyes and looked around. "Oh, well, no, but we can't be that far off the trail. Can we, Nash? We'll just retrace our steps."

Suddenly, Ms. Weston's eyes opened wide. "Oh, wait, there's the call again. Look, class, up there, in that evergreen, flicking its wings. There it is! Oh, oh, how exciting! Isn't this terribly exciting? A ruby-crowned kinglet. They aren't that rare, but as I told you, I don't have one on my list. I always hoped I'd see one, and I knew this trip was my best chance this fall."

Katani wondered how Ms. Weston could be so unconcerned about their predicament when Nash was so clearly worried. He was looking at that map as if it were in ancient Greek.

Suddenly, Chelsea spotted the tiny bird that Ms. Weston was ecstatic about. She thought some extra science points were right there within her grasp. She crept even closer, knelt down, and snapped several photos.

"Oh, Chelsea, you are a perfect wonder. If you got a good photo, we might be able to sell it to some birding magazine. I know at least three that would just die for a good picture."

Hey, science points and money. This was getting better by the minute. Maybe Ms. Weston wasn't crazy after all, figured Chelsea.

Billy Trentini sneezed, and that was the end of the ruby-crowned kinglet, which took off like a shot into the woods. Billy had sneezed it away in an instant. "Sorry, I think I'm allergic to these woods."

"Hey, you might be allergic to kinglets."

"You can get shots for that," Avery said with a straight face.

"Oh, green team, thank you, thank you." Ms. Weston's face lit up with satisfaction. Finding that bird was really a life goal for her. "Now, where were we before I got sidetracked?"

"That's a very good question." Avery looked around.

Nash stood up. "Green team," he announced carefully. "We are definitely lost! Somehow a trail marker has been removed, or fallen. It's possible that the wind that blew through camp last night may have knocked it off. Or sometimes a few really misguided hikers think it's fun to grab a souvenir, and I don't think the rangers have been up here today. In any case, we must have taken a wrong turn."

"But I remember where we went, Nash. Follow me," shouted Avery. And before anyone could stop her she had begun running back down the trail. And then, to everyone's horror ... almost as in a slow-motion movie, Avery went flying through the air like a spinning top and crashed to the ground.

"Trying to be a hero, Madden?" Billy shouted as he raced toward her, followed by Ms. Weston and Nash.

"Great," Maeve whispered to Katani. "We're lost and Avery's acting like one of the Flying Wallendas ... Katani?" Maeve shook her friend's arm.

"Shush, Maeve. I think Avery's hurt ... really hurt. Look," pointed Katani.

CHAPTER 16

❧

PINK SOCKS AND SWAMP THING

THE BLUE TEAM was keeping a good pace, climbing steadily through the trees up the side of the mountain. John whistled softly as he hiked, pausing from time to time to point out different types of vegetation.

Charlotte kept her journal out and wrote furiously every time they stopped on the trail. She wanted to record how it felt to be out in the woods, away from the busy life of school.

"Uh, John?" Joline said hesitantly.

"What's going on?"

"I have to go to the bathroom."

"Alright. Go ahead."

"What do you mean?" Joline asked, looking worried.

"I warned you before. Now it's between you and the woods," John replied, gesturing through the trees.

Joline hesitated for a moment before turning from the path and heading into the woods.

"Although," John added, "I happen to know that we are about five minutes' hike from an old shack that has an outhouse attached to it. Lucky you."

"Uh, OK. Thanks," Joline said, clearly tasting her own sarcastic medicine.

Pete Wexler jogged to the front of the group.

"Hey John, are we going to see any real wildlife? Like mountain lions? Or bears?"

"Mountain lions are only found in twelve western states and Florida—so forget about them. There are black bears in these woods, but I've only seen them a couple of times during the daylight. We'd be more likely to see deer or moose."

"Oh, OK. Thanks, man," Pete said coolly. John sounded like he spent his days reading the encyclopedia.

"What about rattlesnakes?" Isabel asked fearfully.

"The timber rattlesnake is an endangered species in New Hampshire," John explained, "although we are in the woods and you have to be prepared for anything. If you hear a rattle, back away. Snakes only bite as a last resort."

Yikes, Isabel couldn't believe her ears. She wished John would stop relaying nature facts and just climb. She felt safer from snakes when she was moving.

"Alright, we're here," he announced, pointing to a shack about fifty yards off the path. "Betsy, why don't you walk with Joline? It's not far, but I don't want any of you wandering off alone."

Betsy and Joline took off while the others sat down to rest for a few minutes. John passed around some more gorp to refuel the team.

✿

A shriek reverberated through the trees in the otherwise quiet forest. And then silence. Everyone rushed toward Avery, who was lying on the ground—her face white and her eyes closed.

Ms. Weston, her face pale, leaned over her. "Are you alright? Avery, Avery talk to me." Nash sprinkled a little cold water on Avery's face and her eyes began to flutter and she began to moan.

"My ankle. Owwww, it hurts so bad. I think ... I think it might be broken." Avery was clearly trying not to cry, but a couple of tears rolled down her cheek.

Katani and Maeve looked at each other. Avery never cried.

Katani thought the two counselors gave each other that look that said, "This can't be happening."

"Can you move your foot, Avery?" Nash asked, kneeling beside her.

"Great, we get lost in the woods and this loser goes and breaks her ankle," said Kiki, rolling her eyes.

"Hey, Avery is not a loser," said Billy angrily.

"Well, then she shouldn't have run ahead like that," said Anna, who couldn't resist the opportunity to dis one of the BSG.

"It was just an accident," retorted Maeve.

"Quiet, all of you," Nash spoke harshly. "Avery," he asked again, "Can you move your foot?"

Avery shook her head no. "It hurts too much." Avery was trying to be brave in front of the other kids but her ankle was throbbing in pain. And now she felt embarrassed. Anna was right. She shouldn't have been running ahead. Avery felt like a total idiot. She had not followed the hiker responsibility code like she was supposed to.

"Whatever, now we're never going to get back to camp and it's all that dork's fault!" stormed Kiki, pointing at Avery.

Ms. Weston finally noticed the escalating argument. "Kiki, there will be no name-calling on this hike! Avery's in terrible pain and no one wants to hear your negative commentary. If you can't work as part of a team, go sit on that rock over there."

Kiki wasn't ready to let things go just yet.

"Chill out, Ms. Weston. She only tripped over a tree root. Avery's acting like such a drama queen." Kiki turned to make a face at Avery.

There was a shocked gasp from the green team. The Yurmeister's eyes practically bugged right out of his head. Billy Trentini opened his mouth and a big burp came out. Red-faced, he mumbled a quick apology.

Nobody ever talked to teachers like that at Abigail Adams Junior High. They all waited eagerly to see what Ms. Weston would do next. Weston vs. Underwood—no one could guess the outcome.

Ms. Weston stamped her foot and shouted. "Go sit on that rock, Kiki, right now." Kiki hurried over to the rock, realizing that she had gone too far. She didn't even say a word when Anna gave her the "loser" look.

Ms. Weston was obviously at her wit's end. They were lost in the woods, Avery was hurt, and now she felt like she was losing control of her students.

Katani whispered to Maeve, "Ms. Weston is totally mad. I bet she tells my grandmother about this."

Ms. Weston turned her back on Kiki and spoke to the rest of the green team. "This is a serious situation and I need you all to be quiet and stay put while we deal with this. And

... I don't want to see anyone else running. Have I made myself very clear?"

Everyone nodded yes.

Ms. Weston's tirade must have shocked Kiki, because she was completely quiet. Kiki was sitting on the rock, acting like she didn't care, but looking for all the world like a chastised second grader in time-out.

Chelsea Briggs turned away. Kikimania was beginning to get really annoying. They were lost in the woods, for goodness sakes, and Avery Madden had really messed up her foot pretty badly. And still everybody had to focus on Kiki. What was up with that? Chelsea sighed in frustration. Then ... the lightbulb. That's it! Chelsea snapped her finger. She'd figured it out. Kiki had to be the center of attention all the time—everywhere with everyone. If she couldn't get it in a good way, Kiki was going to do whatever it took to bring the attention back to herself ... including insulting other kids with broken feet. Even now. Chelsea saw Kiki out of the corner of her eye pouting as she sat on the rock. Even in a crisis it was the Kiki Show. Chelsea shook her head. That was so screwed up. And they thought she had problems.

Everyone's focus shifted back to Avery. Nash had asked Billy to run back and get his medic pack.

"What do you think, Nash?" asked Ms. Weston.

"Ibuprofen will help bring down the swelling and reduce the pain. I'm not a doctor, so I obviously don't know if her foot is broken or sprained. But both can cause a lot of pain."

"Here, Nash." Billy handed Nash the pack.

The counselor grabbed the bag and opened the compartment with the first aid kit.

Meanwhile, Ms. Weston had managed to get Avery to sit up. The color had begun to return to her face.

Nash handed her some medicine and gave her a sip of water. Ms. Weston gave her a couple of crackers to help wash the dry pills down. Avery gratefully took both.

Nash directed Katani and Yurt to go back to the swamp and soak a bandana with cold water.

"I thought we weren't supposed to separate," Chelsea spoke up.

"You are absolutely correct, but this is an emergency, and I'm going to stand on that rock over there and watch them go. I can see them from there—it's only about fifty yards away. "Get going, guys, and walk—don't run. We have had more than enough trouble for one day."

Avery, who had begun to return to her old self, felt her face flush. Maybe if she tried to stand everything would be all right.

"Avery, how are you feeling?" asked Ms. Weston. "Your face ... you do look a little better." She sounded relieved.

"Yeah, maybe I should try to stand. I think I can ..."

Ms. Weston and Maeve helped her stand, but all her weight was on her good foot. She started to look down at her injured foot.

Maeve, who had Avery by the arm, said, "I don't think you should look, Ave. Your ankle ... it looks like you're hatching a blue dinosaur egg on your foot."

Everyone looked down.

"My," was all Ms. Weston said.

"Cool," said Billy, although he looked a little pale.

"Do you want to try walking, Avery?" Ms. Weston asked, a hint of doubt in her voice.

Avery took a deep breath and tentatively put her injured foot on the ground, but a little yelp of pain escaped her as soon as she put pressure on her foot.

"Avery." Nash, who had left his perch on the rock, said, "You need to get off your feet." Maeve and Ms. Weston helped Avery back to the ground.

At that moment Katani came rushing into the group holding the dripping bandana. Yurt, trailing behind her, was way out of breath and panting.

"Geesh, Summers," he said when he was able to breathe. "You better go out for track when we get back. I've never seen anyone speed walk like that."

"Avery, there is no way we can tell if your foot is broken, so we are just going to have to ice your foot."

Nash took an instant cold pack out and wrapped it around Avery's foot. Then he began wrapping the bandana tightly around Avery's foot. Normally, he wouldn't use a wet bandana, but he had no idea how long they would be out in the woods. The weather was a little warm and he wanted the ice pack to stay cold as long as possible. Plus, the bandana would act as an ace bandage.

"How's that swamp ice feel, kiddo?" he joked.

For the first time since she had fallen, Avery was able to crack a smile.

"Wow, it's return of the swamp thing," cracked Billy Trentini.

Ms. Weston gave him a stern look. He put up his hands quickly. "I was just joking," he apologized.

Maeve rushed to sit down next to her friend. She put her hand on Avery's forehead. "Well," she said optimistically. "At least you don't have a fever." That made Avery giggle.

Nash clapped his hands. "OK, lunch time ... then pow-wow. Everybody get their packs, and Mr. Yurt ..."

The Yurtmeister bowed deeply when he heard the counselor call his name. That completely broke everyone up, even Nash and Ms. Weston.

"What can I do for you my lord?" Henry said in a very royal voice.

"You can go get the pack with all the lunches."

Yurt stood at attention. "Right away, sir." He began to run and then stopped, remembering Ms. Weston's admonition. "Where is the royal lunch pack?"

Nash asked who had been the last person to carry it.

Billy said that he had handed it off to Katani.

Katani said she had handed it off to Chelsea, who said she handed it off to Yurt, who said he handed it off to Maeve, who handed it off to Kiki, who said she thought maybe she had left it by the side of the trail about a half hour earlier when they had stopped to rest. Kiki shrunk from the angry looks of the green team and put her head down. Not a good day for Kiki.

"You lost our lunch?" yelled Billy T. He started to pace in circles. He was starving, having eaten all his gorp on the way through the swamp. In a dramatic gesture worthy of the Yurtmeister, Billy raised his skinny arms to the sky and shouted, "We're all gonna die!" And then he flung himself onto the grass and pounded his fists into the ground. Chelsea knew just how Billy felt.

"Get up, Billy," commanded Nash. He wanted to laugh at Billy's antics, but the counselor could see that the other campers' faces were distressed. It was one thing to be lost and quite another to be lost and hungry.

Ms. Weston gestured to Nash to do something.

Nash blew his whistle. "Everyone sit down. Let the official pow-wow of the green team begin."

As soon as everyone was settled, Nash blew his whistle and said, "Rule #1. Assess the situation."

He pointed at Katani, who thought a minute and chose her words very carefully. "We are lost in the woods with no food. We have an injured camper who can't walk. It's getting late and we are tired and hungry... and very annoyed."

"How about scared," piped in Maeve, who had just brushed off a very creepy looking bug that had settled on Avery's hair.

Nash was impressed with Katani's logical if slightly grim analysis. "Very good, Katani. Now, who wants to take a stab at what we've got going for ourselves."

Dillon raised his hand. Nash gave him the go-ahead.

"We've got water and good weather."

"We are all together," shouted Maeve.

"We're not stupid," Billy piped in.

"We've got counselors who are supposed to know what they are doing," Anna said, looking at Nash with a perfectly innocent face.

"Exactly," he said.

"I saved all my gorp and I have four granola bars and an apple too," offered Chelsea. She had grabbed them from the canteen before she left ... just in case.

Everybody cheered.

"Way to go, Chels." Billy pounded her on the back and sat down next to her, hoping for the first offering.

"That's great. Bring it over here with Ms. Weston's pack of crackers. It will be a veritable feast," Nash winked.

Nash knew that feeding everybody would lighten the mood. So, he spread out his sweatshirt and threw all the food on top. Then he had Chelsea parcel it out so everybody had the same amount. It ended up that each camper got two crackers, a handful of gorp, and a little piece of a granola bar. Some, like Dillon and Yurt, gobbled it immediately. Dillon announced that in a crisis, he felt "immediate gratification was best."

"My mom told me about a health article that said that small amounts of food over time are better than large amounts all at once," Katani told Maeve. "It keeps your energy up."

The two girls decided to adopt that approach to their rations. Chelsea thought it sounded sensible, so she went along with Katani and Maeve.

The ice pack had improved Avery's pain so she was sitting up and munching on the gorp and ready to help with a plan of attack.

"All right," Nash reminded them. "What's the first rule of hiking?"

"Stay together."

Nash gave a thumbs up to the group.

"I think we should go for help. We can make a chair lift for Avery with some of our sweatshirts and tie them to sticks like the Native Americans did," Katani offered in her best Ms. Take Charge voice.

"That's a great idea," Anna said sarcastically. "But if we're lost and don't know where we are supposed to go, where are we going to take her?"

"Anna's right. The second rule of hiking is that you stay where you are and wait for help. Otherwise you just keep getting more and more lost," Nash informed everyone. "We're just going to hunker down and wait. When we don't show up they will send a search party for us."

"But we can't just stay here and wait. It's starting to get cold," whined Anna. "Besides, I heard a noise. I think a bear is tracking us."

"Bears love swampy areas, Anna," Henry Yurt said.

"People step in the mud, get trapped, and then it's easy for a bear to get them. They bring in all their relatives for a feast. Anna-banana casserole."

"You don't put bananas in a casserole," Dillon said. "Even I know that. Anna-banana cake or pie is more like it."

"You're really stupid, Kiki, you know that?" Billy suddenly lost it. "You had one job to do. Pick up the lunch and carry it for what—about ten feet. How could you have lost it?" Billy was still starving. The snack did nothing but whet his appetite for more.

No one had ever seen Billy lose his temper like that. He flopped on the ground beside Avery, ignoring the fact that the ground was pretty damp. The green team was becoming slightly unglued.

Ms. Weston raised her hand in a stop motion. "No use getting mad. It was an honest mistake. What's done is done. None of us is going to starve in the next hour or two," she said firmly.

"I wish everyone would be just be quiet and think of something to do!" Avery shouted. She felt like crying. Even though the cold pack helped, her ankle still hurt and Avery just wanted to go back to her bunk and sleep. She wished that she had stuck Happy Lucky Thingy in her backpack instead of leaving him on her bed. She did not want to stay out here in the woods waiting for a hungry bear. She had had enough adventure.

"I know it's hard ..." began Nash.

Chelsea raised her hand.

"Yes, Chelsea." Nash, ready to lay out his plan, gestured impatiently for Chelsea to speak.

"I think I know how to get back."

All eyes were on Chelsea. Could Chelsea actually have a

solution to their problem? Suddenly, Chelsea Briggs was no longer Chelsea, the helpless gym partner, last to be chosen, first to fall or make a fool of herself. She was Chelsea, their rescuer. The only one smart enough and tough enough to help her classmates out of a bad situation.

"Hey," Nash said in a warmer tone. "I'm all ears. All good ideas are welcome."

Chelsea explained. "When we were walking I was at the back of the line. I built little stone nests along the trail and took pictures of them. I got the idea from a book my brother Ben gave me on hiking in the wilderness. Some hiker did the same thing, and it saved him."

Ms. Weston put her arm around Chelsea and gave her a quick hug.

"What do you think, Nash? Has Chelsea's quick thinking saved the day?"

"Chelsea," the handsome counselor beamed at her. "I think we have a plan."

The wind suddenly picked up and made the trees around them swish and whisper. Nash dashed off with Billy, Dillon, and Yurt to cut down tree saplings. Nash always carried a small ax with him on hikes and now his foresight was proving handy.

Ms. Weston had the rest of the green team dump out their backpacks, and she laid out a patchwork quilt of their sweatshirts.

Chelsea and Maeve knelt down to help tie the sleeves of the sweatshirts together, although they weren't quite sure what was happening next.

"I get it," Maeve marveled. "You are going to tie this to the branches and carry Avery. This is so cool."

"Katani, get my water bottle," directed Ms. Weston.

Chelsea asked Ms. Weston why she needed water.

"You'll see," she smiled slyly.

Katani handed Ms. Weston the bottle of water. Everyone watched as Ms. Weston dampened all the knots.

"That's really cool, Ms. Weston," said Katani. "Now the knots won't slip."

When Nash and the boys came back to camp they were surprised to see that the rest of the team was packed up and ready to go, the blanket ready for Avery's transport.

Avery and Maeve suggested that they tie Maeve's pink socks to the two extra poles. Maeve said it would be kind of like a pink parade through the woods.

Dillon rolled his eyes. He liked Maeve, but she was really kind of girly with all this pink stuff. But Nash thought it was a smashing idea. "There is no pink in the woods, and if somebody sees it they are sure to investigate."

Maeve gave Dillon the cold shoulder. Pink was an important color, Ms. Razzberry Pink had informed her. Too bad for Dillon if he couldn't see that.

Nash and Ms. Weston lowered Avery onto the sweatshirts. When she was comfortable, he gave the order for the porters to line up. Dillon, Katani, and Nash on one side. Ms. Weston, Anna, and Billy on the other. Maeve and Kiki would carry the poles with the pink flags. Chelsea would walk ahead looking for her marks.

Avery yelped as the green team hoisted her into the air. It was a good thing Avery was so light because the saplings were not that wide, and were bending under Avery's weight. When Nash blew his whistle to signal that they should all begin walking, Avery got an attack of the giggles.

"I feel like a pasha from the Arabian Nights."

"Stop laughing, Avery," admonished Anna. "You are making this thing shake like jello."

"I'm not laughing anymore. I'm cold."

"I didn't use a knife to blaze a trail as we were walking," Chelsea told everyone, "but I was really paying attention and taking photos. I was also looking for photo opportunities, so maybe I paid more attention to the trail than some of you did."

"Good thinking, Chelsea," Ms. Weston said approvingly. "Avery, we don't have anything to put over you. We used all the sweatshirts we had. You'll just have to imagine someplace warm."

All of a sudden, Chelsea remembered something. Her brother Ben had given her a space blanket for emergencies. "My brother insisted I bring this." She unfolded it and threw it over Avery.

"Thanks a bunch, Chelsea," Avery said, grateful that somebody had been smart enough to invent the space blanket.

The group continued their trek in what they hoped was the right direction. They passed a big rock that Nash remembered passing on the way in. They began to feel more confident that they had found the right trail home.

Suddenly, Chelsea shouted. "Look. Here's one of my cairns. We're on the right trail."

Nash heaved a sigh of relief, as did every other member

❀

of the green team.

Maeve and Kiki, the pink sock flag bearers, were so excited that they started pumping their flags up in the air.

CHAPTER 17

☙

THE PINK SAFARI

DILLON LAUNCHED into an army-style marching song, making up the words as he walked along.

Chelsea thought of blazing a tree trunk as they walked, but she feared that might scar the tree. Not nice to the tree, Chelsea smiled to herself. Instead, she broke the end of an occasional limb where it hung near the path, then showed Kiki and Maeve how to stack up the few rocks they could find to make their own cairn. Anyone seeing the tiny rock formation would know it wasn't natural. Or if Chelsea was wrong and they were going in the wrong direction again, they could backtrack with no effort.

"How'd you learn how to do all this, Chelsea?" Kiki asked.

"From a book my brother demanded I read before we left. It said that it's usually best to stay put. In fact, they tell little kids to hug a tree and blow their whistle. But I figured that if we could find the trail we made coming in here, we could walk back to the main trail."

Maeve grinned. "I guess brothers can come in handy occasionally, especially older brothers."

❀

"Your brother plays football, doesn't he, Chelsea?" Kiki stopped to pick up a small stone. "What's his name?"

"Ben. People call him Big Ben, for obvious reasons."

Dillon's marching song had caught on, so Kiki, Maeve, and Chelsea joined in. Maeve kept pumping up her pole as though she was the head of a marching band.

"You're in the army now. One, two, buckle my shoe ..." Everybody was singing so loudly that they almost didn't hear the voices.

"Green team!" a ranger shouted. "There you are. We've been looking for you for hours. We just saw your pink socks."

"We were right here." Dillon grinned at their rescuers.

"Man, are we glad to see you guys!" Nash gave the signal to put Avery down.

"You were supposed to walk to Fern Lake," Mia said. "We've been all the way up there and back."

"One of the trail markers must have fallen off or been pulled off. If it hadn't been for Chelsea here, we would be still sitting up in the swamp waiting for you guys ..."

"What have we got here?" The ranger asked as he knelt down next to Avery.

"I think I sprained my ankle, sir."

"Well, I like your entourage."

"Me too."

"Was Fern Lake really beautiful?" Maeve asked Mia. "I did really want to see it."

"Yes, but everything out here is beautiful, don't you think?" Mia smiled.

Chelsea knew she should be starving, but somehow she wasn't. She focused her camera to capture some great shots of light and shadow in the growing darkness as they followed the ranger back to camp.

CHAPTER 18

 os

CAMPFIRE COURAGE

CHARLOTTE HAD just returned from the blue team's hike and was resting by the campfire circle, swigging down an entire bottle of water. She had run out on the way back down the mountain even though she had carried two bottles in her pack. Nick came and sat down and said, "Did you hear? The green team is lost."

Charlotte leaned forward.

"Charlotte. Did you hear me?" Nick turned to follow Charlotte's gaze.

The strangest procession was entering camp, and they were carrying Avery in the oddest contraption Charlotte had ever seen. Of course, Maeve was at the head, acting like she was striding to the beat of a John Phillip Sousa march.

Suddenly, everyone in the camp was running to find out what was going on.

"What happened, Ave?" Charlotte hurried to meet them. "Are you all right?"

Avery waited until Nash placed her in one of the few camp chairs, wincing as she placed a little weight on her foot.

✿

"Oh, nothing," she joked. "I just pulled a Charlotte and became a klutz for about two seconds. Suddenly, bam, I was down. And look what happened!"

"Down and out for the count," Yurt added. "But she's been very patient, letting us carry her all the way back."

Avery grinned at the BSG, who were all gathered around by now.

"Chelsea got us unlost," Katani said to Charlotte. "Turns out she has an excellent sense of direction."

"And a good eye for detail," Billy added, "like which side of the trail the tree moss was on. Tree moss grows on the north."

"Some of the trees were completely covered with moss," Maeve said.

"Lichens," Ms. Weston corrected Billy and Maeve. "The difference between moss and lichen is—"

"Beside the point right now," Jody interrupted and took over. "Has anyone gone for the nurse?"

Isabel had run for the nurse the minute they set Avery down. Everyone watched as Jody unwrapped Avery's soggy foot. Charlotte (who had wiggled her way into the crowd that was now surrounding Avery) gasped. The whole side of Avery's foot was swollen and black and blue.

Charlotte grabbed Avery's hand. "Oh, Avery. That must hurt so badly."

Before Avery could respond, the nurse was there.

"Well, well, what have we got here?"

Avery managed to crack a little smile as the nurse squeezed and turned her ankle carefully.

"Do you think it's broken? I play soccer and basketball, you know. I need my foot."

"You know what? I don't think it's broken. But you do

have one heck of a sprain. When you get back home though, it would be best to have it checked out. Just to be sure."

She wrapped an elastic bandage around Avery's foot and ankle tightly and sent Billy back to the infirmary for crutches. Since they were going home the next morning, the nurse thought that Avery could wait for X-rays until she got home.

Darkness was closing in on them and there was a chill in the air. Jody and her crew had started a roaring fire and, to everyone's delight, had already prepared a dinner of chili, mounds of corn bread, and bowls of coleslaw, with chocolate cupcakes and melon for dessert.

"Everybody ready for a feast?" Jody asked in a big, friendly voice. "You all were awesome today. You all worked liked Clydesdales. And a few of you deserve the 'I climbed Mt. Everest' award. So fuel up, everyone!" Jody looked at Chelsea and grinned when she said that. Chelsea jumped up to join the line that was already forming.

With stomachs full, dishes cleaned up, and the group seated around the campfire with cups of cocoa or hot tea, everyone became exceptionally quiet.

Charlotte thought about how great today's hike up the mountain had been. The climb was challenging, but at the top they were rewarded by a panorama of lakes, fields of grass and reeds, and even more mountains in the distance.

Nick had walked beside her or close to her the entire day. Occasionally he asked Isabel if she was OK, and helped her with her pack and once a blister. But Charlotte realized that that was just how Nick was. If anyone needed help, he was there. She liked him even more because of it. It was as if he'd read one of the BSG's mottos: *Be loyal to each other and give back as much as you take from the universe.*

He sat beside her now, quiet, but very much there. Avery

sat on the other side of Nick, with Billy Trentini on her left. Avery's every wish was their command. She was obviously enjoying her night as Queen of the Camp. Charlotte knew that back home, when Avery was recovering, she'd need her friends even more.

Jody stood and broke the silence. "I hope all of you have had as much fun at Lake Rescue this week as I have. Groups come and go, but this seventh grade from Abigail Adams is among the best I've ever worked with." Jody had to stop talking until everyone got through cheering.

"Yes, congratulate yourselves. I hope all of you will take home wonderful memories and will have learned at least one new thing about yourself ... and a classmate. We're going to start tonight's campfire program by going around and having each one of you tell one thing that surprised you about this week. Who wants to start?"

Maeve jumped up, although no one was required to stand.

"She probably just wants to show off her cute new vest," Katani whispered affectionately to Isabel.

"I didn't want to come, but I've been surprised by how much fun I've had even though one of my best friends got hurt. I enjoyed being outside all week. I especially liked the loons. It's almost as if they are singing a haunting love song."

Maeve and romance, smiled Charlotte, were never far apart.

"Yeah, I thought the trip would be a drag," Dillon said. "I wondered what we'd do if we didn't have a basketball court, but we were busy the entire time."

A lot of other people said they liked being outside and planned to ask their parents if they could go camping next summer.

"Nick," Isabel said, "insisted that I could climb the mountain, then helped me when I had trouble. I surprised myself when I reached the top."

"I realized that sometimes you have to work as a team to get things done." Anna's statement came as a total shock to everyone ... especially Joline, who looked at her friend like she had two heads. Anna just shrugged her shoulders.

"I was surprised by how quickly you can get lost in the woods. I'll never go hiking unless I am really prepared," Dillon said with conviction.

"I learned that you can accomplish much more than you think when you put your mind to it," said a popular girl named Sierra.

"I was surprised at how fast I could walk when I had to." Katani laughed.

"Dude, you surprised me with that too," Yurt joked.

"I learned that you really have to pay attention." Avery's comment got a big laugh.

"Yeah, I have to thank Maeve for thinking pink." Dillon grinned at Maeve.

"When will we get to see your photos, Chelsea?" Yurt asked, and several people chimed in that they wanted to get copies.

"I'll put some of them in the next *Sentinel*, but I can send them around on email," Chelsea offered.

"Thanks to my totally annoying big brother. He made me read a book on what to do if you get lost in the woods." Chelsea grinned.

Once everyone who wanted to had shared, Jody passed around little slips of paper. "Hold on to these until I tell you what they're for," she said. "But now, you're going to have to sit through one more of my little speeches." She paused patiently for everyone to groan, but instead they waited for her to continue. The only sounds were the fire snapping and crackling. Then, as if on cue, the loon called.

Oooo-ooo-oooo-ooo-oooo-ooo.

Everyone giggled until Nick piped in, "That's an augury of a heavy lecture coming, worse than death to sit through."

Jody grinned. "Nick is demonstrating one method of surviving junior high. A sense of humor. I hope all of you have learned to laugh at yourselves this week. If you fell, you picked yourself up, tried again." She looked at Avery. "Unless someone else had to pick you up and carry you in his arms."

Nash reached over and gave Avery a high five.

Avery got poked by an elbow from both sides. She buried her face in her hands until Jody continued.

"I think one of the worst things about being in junior high, about being twelve or thirteen or fourteen, is the fear of 'the big fear.'"

Jody had a rapt audience now. "The fear that I might do something weird and embarrass myself … am I right?"

Everyone nodded in agreement.

Except for Henry Yurt, who stood up and made like a backup dancer for a pop group. The whole group burst into raucous laughter, even Jody.

The Yurtmeister bowed and took his seat.

"I think Henry has just demonstrated, very nicely, I might add, my second point, which is that being embarrassed is not the worst thing in the world."

Now Charlotte got an elbow on either side from Nick and Maeve. She smiled but wanted to keep listening to every word that Jody said.

"So, Jody's rules for having a great life are: Don't sweat the small stuff. We've all got a few hills to climb …" There was a collective groan from her exhausted campers. "Give yourself and each other a break—you are only in seventh grade for goodness' sake. And contrary to seventh grade wisdom, you've all got a few things to learn. Which brings me to my last few recommendations—try new things, learn to get along with all kinds of people. Eat right, and most importantly ..." She turned to Nash and gave him a thumbs up. Suddenly the coolest song in the world came on, and Jody lifted her arms in the air and shouted, "Get a move on!"

With that, the Yurtmeister, the Trentinis, Dillon, and of course Maeve all jumped up to dance. In a split second, the campfire had turned into "Dance Fever." Counselors, kids, chipmunks, and squirrels went wild.

Maeve grabbed Charlotte, who grabbed Katani, who grabbed Dillon, who grabbed Chelsea, who grabbed Yurt, who grabbed Isabel, and on and on until there was a huge conga line snaking its way around the campfire. Sierra, also known to her classmates as "Jazzy," jumped to the front of the conga line and pulled out a "microphone"—aka granola bar—from the pocket of her shorts. She lip-synched the words to the Mariah Carey tune, dancing around the line and holding the microphone in front of her eager backup singers, Brittany, Mandy, Lauren, and Emily. A few of the boys started chanting, "Jazzy! Jazzy!" and everyone else quickly joined in.

Avery, who wasn't big on dancing anyway, sat watching the conga line, cracking up every time Henry broke out into a goofy dance move. Chelsea Briggs thought it was the coolest night of her life.

When the song ended, Jody raised her hand for everyone to take their seats again. Campers sat down near the fire to hear what was next. No one wanted to ruin the moment.

"What I'd like you to do now, as an end to the campfire, is to write down on the little scraps of paper that are being passed around one important thing that you learned about yourself or a friend while you've been at Lake Rescue. You don't have to share it with anyone if you don't want to; just write it down and be proud of yourselves for what you have accomplished here. When you are done, our ritual is to throw the paper into the campfire so your words will remain a part of Lake Rescue forever and inspire future campers."

Maeve loved the drama of that vision and set about earnestly to create something worthy. She wrinkled her brow in concentration.

This was a night of surprises, and Yurt surprised them all. "I have learned that I would like to have a girlfriend," he blurted out.

Jody stared at him while everyone guffawed, especially the boys. "Well, President Yurt, that might be a universal challenge, but be careful what you ask for. You might get it."

Chelsea studied the slip of paper. Finally, she wrote:

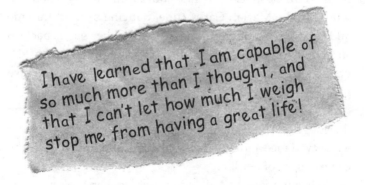

I have learned that I am capable of so much more than I thought, and that I can't let how much I weigh stop me from having a great life!

She added a big exclamation point for emphasis. Chelsea wanted what she wrote to stay with her forever, and she hoped that the next overweight girl who came to camp would experience the same kind of encouragement that she had received here. When it was her turn, she dropped the paper in the fire, watched it flame and blacken. There was something magical about the ashes floating into the sky.

One by one the BSG watched each other drop a note into the fire. They helped Avery get up on her crutches and toss in her slip of paper instead of doing it for her.

For special effects, the loon cried out again, his lovely, haunting melody filling the air.

Without speaking, the campers headed toward the dining hall where the evening would end with a much anticipated dance. A perfect ending to an almost perfect day.

CHAPTER **19**

ભ

A BEARY GOOD NIGHT

AS THE BSG pushed Avery in a wheelchair toward the dining hall—now the dance hall—a loud yell broke the silence of the campfire.

Suddenly, Henry Yurt sprinted by shouting, "Live bear! Live bear!"

"He's not kidding." Nick followed Yurt, grabbing Charlotte's arm as he ran close to her. She scrambled to keep up with him.

"Help, help, it really is a bear!" Dillon brought up the rear. "Run, climb a tree, get inside, something!"

Sure enough, a big black animal chased behind the boys. With no time to do anything, the rest of the girls huddled together and watched it lumber by, long black ears flopping beside its huge head.

"Wait a minute," Avery said. "Bears don't have long, floppy ears."

"Or long wagging tails," Katani added.

The "bear" turned, letting the boys escape, and ran toward the girls. He jumped up on Isabel, knocking her flat.

"Help, help me, he's slobbering all over me!" Isabel screamed.

Katani, Maeve, and Avery doubled over with laughter. Taking pity on Isabel, Maeve pulled what looked like an enormous black dog off of her.

"What kind of dog is this big?" she asked, staring at the dog, whose tongue lolled over the edge of her mouth while it waited eagerly for the girls to pet it. Thump, thump. "Yikes," murmured Katani. "That's the loudest tail wag I've ever heard." Then she backed away, not quite sure that this actually was a dog and not a strange animal found only in the wilds of New Hampshire.

"A Newfoundland. She's a Newfoundland," Avery said. "Where did she come from?"

"She must be lost. Does she have a collar and tags?" Isabel said, then started laughing. "Ave, you're a lost dog magnet. But this one is twenty times the size of Marty. We could never hide *her* in Charlotte's attic."

The boys and Charlotte walked slowly back to where the girls were taking turns petting the bear/dog.

"Here's your girlfriend, Yurt," Avery teased. "Be careful what you wish for."

"No tags, no way to find her owner. She's all yours, Yurt." Maeve collapsed in laughter again.

"You'll have to give her a bath before she can ride on the bus, though, and she's not sitting by me." Isabel was still brushing off wet leaves and combing twigs from her hair. "Look at me. These were the nicest clothes I brought. I saved them for the dance."

Yurt, Nick, and Dillon wore very sheepish looks. "It was dark," Yurt said. "How could I see that it was a dog?"

"Yeah, we've all been told to be on the lookout for bears.

Our imaginations just ran away from us." Dillon knelt down and hugged the Newfoundland, letting her lick his face. "Are you lost, girl? President Yurt here loves lost causes."

"Well, up until now, I hadn't felt embarrassed and stupid this week. But I guess this takes care of it." Nick grinned. "We can go home now."

"We can go home tomorrow," Charlotte reminded him. "We were on our way to a dance, remember?"

At the word dance, the Newfie stood up, placing her paws on Yurt's shoulders. She was as tall as he was, but not quite as skinny, despite being out in the woods alone.

"OK, OK, if you insist." Yurt took both paws in his hands and stepped back and forth with the huge dog, looking for all the world like a clown in the circus with a trained bear.

"Anyone who would teach a dog this big a trick must love her a lot," Avery surmised. "We have to find her owners. Maybe they are camping someplace out here."

"I'll tell John to send out a lost dog alert," Nick suggested. "We don't want to miss the dance."

Yurt named the dog "Ursula" and got her to follow him to the camp office. Someone was always there to answer phones, treat cuts and bruises, or solve problems. Ursula trotted alongside Yurt as if she'd known him forever.

They all stumbled into the dining hall, still cracking up about Henry's new girlfriend. A few other campers had heard the commotion and wanted to know what had happened.

Since Avery was confined to a chair, the rest of the BSG let her be the storyteller. Dillon grabbed Maeve and slid onto the dance floor.

Billy pulled Isabel into the crowd, knowing Avery couldn't do much dancing with her injury ... and probably would refuse to dance with him anyway.

Katani's face registered surprise when Josh Trentini grabbed her hand and challenged her to keep up with him.

"I would try to save you from a real bear." Nick's eyes twinkled at Charlotte.

"Yeah, you'd shimmy up the tree first, then reach back to pull me up, if I hadn't already been eaten." Charlotte would rather tease Nick than be serious.

Then the loudest rock and roll song came on and the whole dance floor seemed to go wild. Charlotte was taken up in a group of girls, and Kiki Underwood grabbed Nick .

A few members of the green and blue teams were standing by the refreshment table when Chelsea walked up.

"Chelsea, when we get back, I'm going to help you figure out how to make money with this photography business of yours, and then you'll have enough to buy a movie camera." Katani handed Chelsea a lemonade and leaned down to rub her foot, the foot that Josh had managed to step on. "Course, you missed the best scene, but maybe we can reenact it for a seventh-grade film festival."

"Yeah, Yurt found a dance partner out in the wilderness," Avery said, reaching across her wheelchair to poke him in the arm.

"No way did I miss that." Chelsea grinned. "Didn't you see my flash go off? I don't know whether to use that dancing bear shot for blackmail or as the first photo in the next *Sentinel*."

"Go ahead, use it." Yurt snatched a cookie. "I'm going to be the most famous seventh-grade president Abigail Adams has ever had. And I did my good deed, like any politician would. Mike from the camp office said that Ursula belongs to an old man who lives along the road into camp. Mike's driving her back home right now."

"You can retire for the rest of the year," Charlotte said.

"Oh, no, I have a lot of great ideas left." The Yurtmeister had recovered from the bear scare and was already thinking about how to use it to his advantage. He turned around and bumped into Anna.

Anna grinned. "Yurt has been taking dancing lessons, just to get ready for tonight. Come on, Yurt, show us what you got." Anna pulled a red-faced Yurt into the crowd.

"Well, I'll have to say, Anna Banana is lots less clumsy than the Newfie," Billy noticed as he sat out the next dance with Avery.

"Life is full of surprises," Chelsea said. "That's what I've learned this week."

Nick surprised Chelsea. "Want to dance, Chelsea?"

Chelsea blushed. Nick Montoya was asking her to dance. He was just being nice, she thought sadly. Then she realized. Yeah, he was being nice … to her. And he didn't even have to.

"Thanks, Nick, but I have to take pictures. Maybe another time. Look at Yurt and Anna. Is that the Swim or the Wiggle?"

"Both," he grinned.

Chelsea passed up the plates of cookies, both hands attached to her camera. Charlotte watched as she worked her way around the room, snapping photos.

Suddenly, Nick decided it was time for a fast dance. He pulled Charlotte onto the dance floor. Charlotte struggled to keep up with his expert moves. When they got home, she'd have to ask Maeve to give her some dance lessons. It was so embarrassing to dance with a boy who was a better dancer than you.

಼

CHAPTER 20

THE PEOPLE ON THE BUS GO HOME

CHARLOTTE DIDN'T think she could sleep at all Thursday night, but by the time Nick walked her, Isabel and Chelsea home from the dance—to protect them from bears, he said— she was so exhausted she could hardly put on her pajamas. She thought that she would dream of Nick, but the next thing she knew someone was walking around the cabins, ringing a bell, way too early.

"Oh, I could sleep for a week." Isabel sat up and yawned.

"Me too." Charlotte groaned and turned over. "What time is it?"

"Six a.m." Chelsea grinned. "Maybe we can just pile onto the bus and sleep all the way home."

"I need a shower." Charlotte pulled on yesterday's dirty clothes.

"We all smell the same." Isabel stuffed clothes into her pack, not even trying to fold them neatly, just making sure she had everything.

Breakfast included cocoa in take-away cups and bagels that they could eat on the bus. The drivers wanted to get home before rush hour traffic.

Chelsea looked around for her favorite counselor and made a beeline for her. Chelsea was not going to miss out on thanking the person who had made this one of the best experiences she had ever had. "Jody, thank you so much," Chelsea said. "I think you've changed my life."

Jody put her arms around Chelsea and gave her a big hug. "For the better, I hope. Promise you'll email me. I want to know how you're doing. Really. And don't forget those photos."

Charlotte, standing next to them, realized that Chelsea had formed a lasting bond with Jody. Charlotte felt closer to all her friends, and to a few other classmates, like Chelsea, who she hadn't known well before the week's activities. Mrs. Fields had been right. Lake Rescue had opened up new doors for everyone.

Waving out the windows, the BSG watched their counselors fade into the fabric of Lake Rescue.

"Thank you for not letting me stay home," Maeve said, sipping her cocoa and stuffing the rest of her bagel and cream cheese into her mouth.

"You really didn't want to come?" Dillon sat in front of her, beside Billy Trentini, but he was turned around so he could talk with Maeve.

Maeve shook her head while she swallowed. "I thought I'd hate every minute of it."

"I loved every minute until I met that root." Avery had a whole seat to herself so she could prop up her leg. "Cross your fingers, guys, that I'll be ready for basketball."

"I can teach you to play backgammon," Billy offered.

"Oh, goody. I know I'd love sitting around playing board games, or rather 'bored' games." She opened her mouth wide for a pretend yawn. Maeve winced. Here was Billy trying to be nice and typical Avery dissed him. Maeve gave her friend a kick on her good ankle. Avery looked like she was going to yell, but Maeve's face made Avery realize that she had been a little too dismissive of Billy.

"Ah, thanks, Billy. Maybe we can play backgammon. I'd love to beat you."

Maeve groaned. Avery would never change. But Billy didn't seem to mind. He high-fived her and went back to tormenting the Yurtmeister.

Charlotte was trying to stay awake, afraid if she slept she'd snore, or worse, fall over and drool. Maybe she could make a pillow of her jacket and lean on the window.

"It's just like Jody told us," Maeve said as she turned to speak to Charlotte. "We were all afraid that we couldn't do all the activities and we'd make fools of ourselves."

"Yeah, but we didn't," Katani said, "except for Yurt and his new doggie friend."

"I heard that." Yurt's head popped up. "The Yurtmeister never falters or folds under stress, even when having to dance with bears. I hope Ursula found her own way home."

"Like Marty did." Avery smiled, and memories of hiding Marty, all his antics, tricks, and majorly cute ways, flowed through all the Beacon Street Girls' minds.

"Remember how Marty ran out into the audience at the talent show?" Isabel asked. "I thought we'd lost him for sure. Thought we'd all get sent home for bringing a dog to the theater."

"Not by my dad," Maeve said. "He loves dogs."

After rehashing the week, everyone dozed off. If anyone was awake, they were quiet, writing in journals or thinking about their adventures.

❋

When the bus arrived back at school, students collected their bags and searched for their parents in the parking lot.

"When are we getting together?" Katani said. "I need a makeover from Maeve, new nail polish ..."

"I need to see Marty." Avery struggled with her things until Billy grabbed her bags along with his.

"Look, Ave, there's your Mom and Scott. She looks really worried. Wave so she knows you're still alive." Billy picked up Avery's hand and waved it out the window.

"Trentini, you are ridiculous."

"I know, but don't you love me anyway?" he beamed. His twin, Josh, picked up Avery's backpack. "Mom said hurry. You need a hand, Avery?"

"No, thanks. Here comes Scott."

Avery's brother had climbed on the bus and was heading toward his sister. "Nice work, Ave," he said with a grin as he grabbed her under one arm.

Charlotte spotted her dad walking toward her, a big smile on his face.

"I want to hear everything that happened," Mr. Ramsey said, giving his daughter a big hug. "I have pizza in the car; I figured you'd be tired of camp food."

"Actually camp food wasn't too bad." Charlotte climbed into the car for the short ride home. But the smell of cheese and pepperoni made her hungry, and she was eager to share every minute of the week with her father. Well, almost every minute.

She looked up to see Nick waving at her. He was already starting home. His parents had to work and couldn't pick him up. Some kids might feel bad about that, but not Nick. Montoya's Bakery was a family affair.

"Want a ride?" she offered.

He shook his head. "I need to stretch my legs. See you tomorrow?"

Charlotte smiled and nodded.

"That boy seems to like you, Charlotte." Mr. Ramsey kept his eyes on the road. "Am I right?"

"Maybe." Charlotte blushed. She had so much to write about in her journal, she could hardly wait.

Charlotte's Journal

I worried so much about finding a best friend at Abigail Adams, it never occurred to me that I might meet a friend who's a boy. It was really fun hanging out with Nick this week and getting to know him better ... he's really nice to everyone, and especially to me.

This week of being outside most of the time, even in the rain, really made me look forward to camping with my dad next summer. I'm going to hold him to his idea that we go someplace together. We can spend the winter making plans.

Maybe we can visit some of the places that he and Mom travelled to. I would really like that.

Avery's Blog

Well, I have really done it now. How could I be clumsy enough to fall over a root? But I did, and my ankle hurts. It's not broken, but it may take weeks to heal. Here's my plan:

1. *Try not to be a crybaby. All athletes get an injury sometime.*

2. *Find something else I like to do while I heal.*
3. *What else do I like to do besides sports?*
4. *I guess I could study.*
5. *Learning to play backgammon with Billy might be fun.*
6. *I could teach Marty some cool new tricks.*
7. *Maybe I should be like my mom and get involved with a charity or something. That would be OK as long as I don't have to cook. At least it would take my mind off of all the sports I'm missing. Hope this doesn't last long!*

* *

Maeve's Notes to Self:

1. Ask Dad to take Sam and me camping next summer.
2. Ask Dillon to go to a movie, but ask Charlotte and Nick to go with us, and let the guys choose the flick. But what about Riley? I hope he feels better. He's going to be so sorry he missed this.
3. Stop judging people by the way they look. Getting to know Chelsea this week made me realize that even though I was never mean to her, I did kind of ignore her ...
4. Find some time for Sam each week. But, I absolutely refuse to play army. That is beyond the call of duty. I suppose he won't let me give him a makeover.

Isabel's Diary

I can't believe I didn't want to go to Lake Rescue! I had such a great time, and I'm going to make a list of all the things I did that scared me, that I thought I couldn't do. Then, when I get scared to do something, I'll look back at the list and remind myself of trying and succeeding. Nick was so nice to me all week, helping me whenever I needed it. I like him, but so does Charlotte, and I'd never flirt with him. The most important thing I did was to fill my journal with drawings of flowers and trees, and the small lake where the loon lived. I'll do a watercolor of the loon for Mama's birthday.

P.S. And I didn't even see one spider! :)

Kgirl List:

1. Surprise everyone at dinner and tell them I love camping!
2. Research cool camp clothes.
3. Send Chelsea more ideas about managing her business. Think she should send the funny photo of Yurt dancing with Ursula to a New Hampshire newspaper.
4. Plan amazing science project.

Chelsea Briggs'

PERSONAL, SUPER-PRIVATE JOURNAL

NO TRESPASSING ... Ever!

I am permanently banishing the word fat from my vocabulary. And if it comes back I am throwing it in the wastebasket. What a waste of energy thinking about my weight. I want to have fun! At camp people seemed to like me. Nick Montoya, one of the coolest boys in the school, asked me to dance, and he wasn't doing it to make fun of me. Maybe next time I'll even take him up on his offer. And Billy Trentini told me I was awesome for standing up to Kiki Underfabulous. That was totally cool. Although I am not going to call her that again. Name-calling is a loser thing to do. I don't like it ... nobody does. Kiki did make me so mad though.

This week was full of firsts: first time I tried so many scary things, like climbing up that rock wall. Even if I didn't make it to the top, I tried. And diary—can you believe it—I got us all un-lost. I'll have to thank Ben every day for the rest of my life for making me read that book. But I used my common sense, too, and I do have a good eye for detail because of my photography. Never knew that until now.

I think I got some great photos. Charlotte said that they'd be the hit of The Sentinel *this month. I think if people started thinking of me as the girl who takes awesome photos instead of the girl who is so fat she can't do anything in gym, I could have a new reputation.*

Jody was so great to talk to. I'm going to email her. I won't be like a nuisance or a stalker or anything. I'll just tell her what I'm doing. And I'm going to make a list of things I want to try once I've lost some weight. I'm not getting on a scale—nooo! to scales. But I already feel lighter.

Maybe I'll learn to dance. Maybe Ben will help me. As big as he is, he's an awesome dancer. I remember once he was dancing by himself in the kitchen, practicing for the prom, and Mom came in. He grabbed her and made her dance with him. She was laughing so hard, she kept stepping on his feet.

I have another idea. I'm going to ask my mom if she will exercise with me. Jody said try to find a partner so you keep each other motivated. We can join a gym, and go when she gets home from work. We don't have to go to some fancy-shmancy ranch, but we can make it part of our everyday activities. Maybe we can even cook some stuff we both like.

Mom's always hinting that I should go to a fat (oops!) —weight management camp :-) in the summer. But that's not my style. I want to go to an Outward Bound camp for teens. She'll think that will be too hard, but when I tell her what I did at Lake Rescue she will be so amazed, I know she'll let me do it.

Chelsea Briggs
— soon to be famous wildlife and nature photographer.
Grrr!

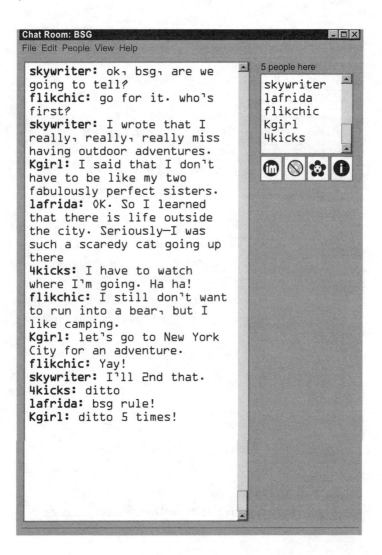

Chat Room: BSG

File　Edit　People　View　Help

skywriter: ok, bsg, are we going to tell?
flikchic: go for it. who's first?
skywriter: I wrote that I really, really, really miss having outdoor adventures.
Kgirl: I said that I don't have to be like my two fabulously perfect sisters.
lafrida: OK. So I learned that there is life outside the city. Seriously—I was such a scaredy cat going up there
4kicks: I have to watch where I'm going. Ha ha!
flikchic: I still don't want to run into a bear, but I like camping.
Kgirl: let's go to New York City for an adventure.
flikchic: Yay!
skywriter: I'll 2nd that.
4kicks: ditto
lafrida: bsg rule!
Kgirl: ditto 5 times!

5 people here

skywriter
lafrida
flikchic
Kgirl
4kicks

To be continued ...

sneak preview!

BOOK 7: freaked out COMING SOON!

ALSO AVAILABLE AT:

www.beaconstreetgirls.com and **www.amazon.com!**

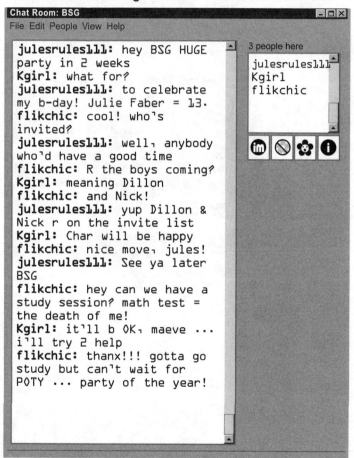

```
Chat Room: BSG                                    _ □ X
File Edit People View Help

  julesrules111: hey BSG HUGE        3 people here
  party in 2 weeks                   julesrules111
  Kgirl: what for?                   Kgirl
  julesrules111: to celebrate        flikchic
  my b-day! Julie Faber = 13.
  flikchic: cool! who's
  invited?
  julesrules111: well, anybody        🔵 🚫 🌸 ℹ️
  who'd have a good time
  flikchic: R the boys coming?
  Kgirl: meaning Dillon
  flikchic: and Nick!
  julesrules111: yup Dillon &
  Nick r on the invite list
  Kgirl: Char will be happy
  flikchic: nice move, jules!
  julesrules111: See ya later
  BSG
  flikchic: hey can we have a
  study session? math test =
  the death of me!
  Kgirl: it'll b OK, maeve ...
  i'll try 2 help
  flikchic: thanx!!! gotta go
  study but can't wait for
  POTY ... party of the year!
```

Check it out:

www.beaconstreetgirls.com

**THE NEW TOWER RULES
CREATED BY THE NEWEST ORDER
OF THE RUBY AND THE SAPPHIRE**

Be it resolved that *all* girls are created equal!

1. We will speak our minds, but we won't be like obnoxious or anything.
2. We won't put ourselves down, even if we aren't super-smart, super-coordinated, or a supermodel.
3. We'll be loyal to our friends and won't lie to them even if they make a mistake or do something totally embarrassing.
4. We will go for it—how will we know what we can do if we don't try?
5. We will try to eat healthy and stay active. How can you chase your dream if you can't keep up?
6. We won't just take from people and the planet. We'll try to give back good things too.

☙ .... ❧

Amendments:

1. We can add as many amendments as we like.
2. We will dare to be fashion individualistas—like we're all different so why should we dress the same?
3. Sometimes we'll veg out—just because we feel like it!
4. We should have as much fun as we can.
5. We should try to save money so if we ever want to we can start a business or something someday.
6. We will try to keep an open mind about new people.
7. When in doubt ... phone home!
8. We won't let people take advantage of us ... we deserve respect!
9. We won't let competition ruin the BSG— friendship is way more important than winning.

Note from Charlotte
Proposed new amendment:
10. We won't judge people by their looks.

What's the vote?
Maeve—fantabulous plan.
Katani—good idea.
Avery—I'm in!
Isabel—let's do it.

10 Questions for You and Your Friends to Chat About

1. How do you think Chelsea feels when other kids make fun of her?

2. Why does Isabel get so upset about her cartoon?

3. Why is it important not to judge people by the way they look?

4. Do you think it was right for Chelsea to call Kiki "Ms. Kiki Underpants?"

5. Have you ever felt pangs of jealousy like Charlotte? How did you get over it?

6. What are the key things to remember to lead a healthy lifestyle?

7. How did each of the BSG change during their trip to Lake Rescue?

8. What were some of the brave things that the Abigail Adams Jr. High kids did while they were at Lake Rescue?

9. Have you ever gone on a trip that changed your life?

10. What were three important lessons that the BSG and their classmates learned at Lake Rescue?

✿

Charlotte's Word Nerd Dictionary

Spanish Words & Phrases

Hola: (p. 2) interjection—hello.
Amigas: (p. 2) noun—friends.
Muy loca: (p. 3)—very crazy.
Deseas Venir: (p. 43)—Do you want to come?
Hija: (p. 44) noun—daughter.
Muy Bonita: (p. 44)—very beautiful.
Buena: (p. 45) adjective—good.
Chicas: (p. 52) noun—girls.

Other Cool Words ...

Nonchalance: (p. 14) noun—not caring.
Aplomb: (p. 15) noun— confidence.
Ratifying: (p. 16) verb—formally establishing an important law.
Enlightened: (p. 17) adjective—in the know.
Perils: (p. 22) noun—really dangerous stuff ... beware!
Tantamount: (p. 28) equal to.
Shazam: (p. 36) exclamation—BOOM! ... just like that.
Methodically: (p. 60) adverb—in an orderly way.
Pungent: (p. 75) adjective—really strong smelling or tasting.
Odyssey: (p. 100) noun—an adventurous trip.
Unrepentant: (p. 118) adjective—not sorry.
Augury: (p. 123) noun—warning.
Belay: (p. 130) verb—to make a rope really secure (essential for climbing rock walls or real mountains!).
Ravine: (p. 135) noun—a deep valley.
Wryly: (p. 147) adverb—with sarcasm.

Refuge: (p. 150) noun—a place to go when you're in trouble.

Catastrophe: (p. 157) noun—complete disaster.

Tremolo: (p. 160) noun—notes, sung by a person or a bird, that sound like they are shaking or vibrating.

Reverent: (p. 161) adjective—respectful.

Gorp: (p. 176) noun—mix of peanuts, raisins, dried fruit, M&Ms, or other foods that increase your energy.

Reverberated: (p. 188) verb—echoed.

Chastised: (p. 190) verb, adjective—yelled at.

Cairn: (p. 201) noun—tiny rock formation.

Lichen: (p. 204) noun—fungus that grows on rocks and trees.

Panorama: (p. 205) noun—beautiful view of things like trees, the ocean, and really cool buildings.

Raucous: (p. 208) adjective—noisy and uncontrollable.

Rehashing: (p. 219) verb—telling a story again.

❀

1. What yummilicious treat does Charlotte bring home to her dad from Montoya's Bakery?
   A. A double chocolate frosted brownie
   B. Lemon squares
   C. Biscotti
   D. Strawberry shortcake

2. Who rescues Maeve from falling off the rope climb?
   A. The Yurtmeister
   B. Nick
   C. Riley
   D. Dillon

3. What is Chelsea Briggs' job at Lake Rescue?
   A. Chief Birdwatcher
   B. Official Photographer
   C. Head Dishwasher
   D. Lead Storyteller

4. Which is NOT on Chelsea's list of mean things to do to the Queens of Mean?
   A. Tip over their canoe
   B. Make A & J walk through poison ivy
   C. Take unflattering pictures of them
   D. Squirt whipped cream in their hands while they're sleeping

5. What prize do the BSG win on Pajama Day?
   A. A night of bowling at Stardust Lanes
   B. Gift certificate to Filene's Basement
   C. An edible fruit basket
   D. Gift certificate to Burger Barn

6. What BSG, besides Charlotte, does Nick have his eye on at Lake Rescue?
   A. Katani
   B. Maeve
   C. Isabel
   D. Avery

7. What kind of bird makes really spooky ghost noises?
    A. Bluebird
    B. Sparrow
    C. Duck
    D. Loon

8. Who gets hurt on the big hike?
    A. Maeve
    B. Avery
    C. Kiki
    D. Chelsea

9. Who is the Yurtmeister's dance partner at Lake Rescue?
    A. Katani
    B. Betsy Fitzgerald
    C. Isabel
    D. Ursula, the dog

10. What is one of Charlotte's biggest fears?
    A. Heights
    B. Moving
    C. Spiders
    D. Hurricanes

(Answers right below!)

· ·

SCORING

8—10 Points: Congrats ... You're a Beacon Street Girl at heart!
We can never have too many BFFs!

5—7 Points: Nice work ... How 'bout we hang out at
Montoya's after school?

0—4 Points: No problem ... let's go get some Swedish Fish!

· ·

ANSWERS: 1. C. Biscotti **2.** D. Dillon **3.** B. Official Photographer **4.** D. Squirt whipped cream in their hands while they're sleeping **5.** A. A night of bowling at Stardust Lanes **6.** C. Isabel **7.** D. Loons **8.** B. Avery **9.** D. Ursula, the dog **10.** B. Moving

CR

BEACON STREET GIRLS®

fun, easy, and totally healthy ...

HEALTHY *you!*

Yummy!

Check out our recipes!

turn the page for cool, healthy stuff

HEALTHY *you!*

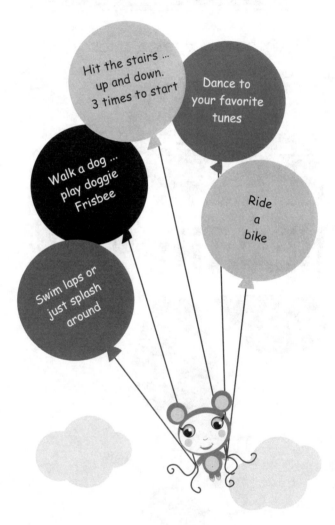

- Hit the stairs ... up and down. 3 times to start
- Dance to your favorite tunes
- Walk a dog ... play doggie Frisbee
- Ride a bike
- Swim laps or just splash around

Get a move on!

Catch Some Zzzzzzzz ...

Do you yawn your way through first period? Or totally lose your energy in the afternoon? You're probably not getting enough sleep. Kids should get AT LEAST nine hours of snooze time every night. Studies show that getting enough sleep improves your grades, too. If you have trouble falling asleep, listen to some quiet music or take a hot bubble bath and then crawl under the sheets ... you'll be dreaming in no time!

Take a Deep Breath and CHILLAX ...

Feeling stressed out? Time to take a break. Take a few deep breaths to get some oxygen to your brain. Yoga is a really fun way to clear your mind, and it's great for your muscles and flexibility, too. Turn off the TV and pick up a book. Take a walk and enjoy the scenery. Life is busy ... slow down and enjoy it.

How to Stay Healthy

Nix the tube ...

Watching too much TV gets in the way of living a healthy lifestyle. It's easy to develop poor snacking habits when you're hooked on your favorite show, and exercise flies out the window once you've settled on the couch for the evening. Limit your TV watching so you have time to do the stuff that really counts ... reading, playing games, hanging out with your friends and family, and getting a move on!

Go for Water~H2O~ Agua~L'eau~Wasser~ Acqua ...

Are you thirsty? Then you're already dehydrated. Drink water throughout the day to stay healthy and give your body the nutrients it needs. Keep a bottle in your backpack, and don't forget to bring extra water to sports or dance class. If you think plain water is boring, try the flavored kind.

HEALTHY *you!*

5 Important Food Facts

I love to cook!

1 Food looks good, tastes good, and keeps you healthy.

2 Too much of anything—even the healthy stuff—can give you a stomachache.

3 Fruits and veggies are not the enemy.

4 Never give up carbs or fats, even if you've heard it's a good idea ... you need all the food groups to keep you healthy, strong, happy, and full of energy.

5 Food is fun— try a new recipe every week.

Chelsea Briggs' Healthy Snacks

Applelicious!

If you like the taste of a crisp and juicy McIntosh, Granny Smith, or Red Delicious apple, you will adore these creative apple toppers … a healthy and yummy after-school or anytime treat! Try eating cold apple slices with any of the following delights:
- cheddar cheese
- peanut butter
- cinnamon (and a little sugar!)
- cottage cheese

If you're feeling adventurous, add a few apple slices to a tossed salad or your favorite sandwich … the crunch is unbelievably tasty.

English Muffin Pizzas

What you need:
- 1 English muffin
- 2 tablespoons tomato sauce
- 2 slices low-fat mozzarella cheese

What to do: Pull apart the muffin into two halves. Spread tomato sauce evenly on each half. Place slice of cheese on each half. Make sure an adult knows you're about to use the oven and is available for help! Put the mini pizzas on a sheet of tin foil and bake for 5-8 minutes, or until the cheese melts. With oven mitts, carefully remove your pizzas. Let them cool for a minute, then take a bite out of your masterpiece!

Frozen Grapes

The perfect snack when you crave something cool and refreshing …

Instructions: Rinse and dry a bunch of green or red seedless grapes. Pluck the grapes from the vine, place them in a bowl, and put the bowl in the freezer. Wait about two hours, pull the frozen grapes out, and enjoy this healthy treat.

✿

HEALTHY *you!*

TOP TEN TIPS FOR A HEALTHIER YOU!

From Lilian Cheung, D.Sc., R.D.,
Director of Health Promotion & Communication,
Harvard School of Public Health
and Mavis Jukes, teacher and best-selling co-author:
Be Healthy! It's a Girl Thing: Food, Fitness, and Feeling Great.

1. Only watch your favorite TV shows—a couple of shows each day, tops.
2. When you go out for fast food, choose from the healthy side of the menu—salads or sandwiches instead of Big Macs and fries.
3. Fast Food Employee: "Would you like to super-size your meal?"
    You: "No, thank you."
4. Join a sports team, outdoor club, or dance class at your school or in your town.
5. Drink low-fat or skim milk. Healthier than whole milk, and still creamy.
6. Ask your parents to buy whole-grain bread ... more taste and very filling.
7. Eat lots of fruits and vegetables. A glass of fruit juice is OK, but whole fruits are better.
8. Regular mealtimes are the way to go: breakfast, lunch, dinner, and a couple of healthy snacks in between. This is a plan you can stick to.
9. Get involved at school—ask for nutritious snacks in the vending machine. Talk to your gym teachers about playing games that get the whole class involved.
10. Limit unhealthy foods and drinks like soda, sugary desserts, fatty meats, butter, sugary cereals, white potatoes, white rice, white pasta, and white bread.

Need Help Getting Healthy?

1. Ask your pediatrician for help.
   They're trained to help kids get healthy.

2. Check out the book *Dealing with the Stuff That Makes Life Tough: The 10 Things That Stress Girls Out and How to Cope with Them* by Jill Zimmerman Rutledge, or hit your local bookstore or library for information.

3. Keep a journal. When you write down your goals, you are more likely to achieve them.

web sites

Check these out!

www.kidshealth.org/kid
www.4girls.gov
www.bam.gov
www.girlsinc.com

Good Luck!

BOOK 1

worst enemies/best friends
by annie bryant

*Worst Enemies/
Best Friends*

BOOK 2

bad news/good news
by annie bryant

*Bad News/
Good News*

BOOK 3

letters from the heart
by annie bryant

*Letters From
The Heart*

BOOK 4

out of bounds
by annie bryant

Out Of Bounds

BOOK 5

promises, promises
by annie bryant

Promises, Promises

BOOK 6

lake rescue
by annie bryant

Lake Rescue

**COMING SOON
(2006)**

Book 7 - *Freaked Out*
Book 8 - *Lucky Charm*

"I went to the bookstore and BOOM! I just found the best book in the world."

~Taryn, 10